The Botticelli Caper

Donning her magnifying v   face. Rembrandt's palette included sever   .ead white, bone black, charcoal black, och   .ite, yellow lake, and vermillion. What she could see didn't match those on the Rembrandts she had reviewed on the way back from the murder scene.

She stood and invited Armani to take her place. "Take a look."

He sat and peered through the visor. "I don't like any of the colors, but the green is weird."

"I agree. These don't look like Rembrandt's usual choices. And some of the varnish looks recent as well—no yellowing."

They changed places.

She focused on the edges of the canvas. No telltale swatches of paint on two sides. But the third and fourth sides revealed trial patches of paint that matched the colors in the quadrant she found suspicious.

"Uh-oh."

"What?"

Then she saw the tiny happy face; it was the same graffito she'd found on the Botticelli.

"It's another forgery. By the same artist who painted the fake Botticelli."

He eyed her soberly. "I remember, Miss Flora, that you said once you thought forgeries should be on view along with authentic pieces, to provide education for visitors and students of art history."

Flora smoothed her curly hair with shaking hands. "That might be appropriate in a university art gallery, but I'm not sure the Uffizi would ever agree to do that. And I think forgeries should never be displayed for a long time—it gives them too much prominence."

"Correct. Tourists come to Firenze from far away to see original paintings. They'd feel cheated if they discovered they were looking at forgeries. And our dear director will not be happy about this new fiasco."

"He'll go ballistic."

"I will accompany you to tell him. That way his wrath will fall on both of us, not just you."

"That's kind of you, Federico. Thanks."

What They Are Saying About

The Botticelli Caper

About *Burnt Siena*, the first book in the Flora Garibaldi Art History Mystery series:

The author of the Lisa Donahue Archaeological Mysteries launches a new series that provides the perfect antidote for mystery buffs who still miss Iain Pears's mysteries featuring British art dealer Jonathan Argyll.

—Library Journal

About *Catacomb*, the second book in the Flora Garibaldi Art History Mystery series:

Dr. Wisseman's extensive archaeological experience produces vivid and accurate descriptions as clues in a recovered diary guide her characters deeper into murky subterranean tunnels filled with danger and intrigue.

—Marie Moore
Author of The Sidney Marsh Murder Mystery Series

The Botticellli Caper

Sarah Wisseman

A Wings ePress, Inc.
Mystery Novel

Wings ePress, Inc.

Edited by: Jeanne Smith
Copy Edited by: Joan C. Powell
Executive Editor: Jeanne Smith
Cover Artist: Trisha FitzGerald-Jung

All rights reserved

Wings ePress Books
www.wingsepress.com

Copyright © 2019 by: Sarah Wisseman
ISBN 978-1-61309-608-6

Published In the United States Of America

Wings ePress Inc.
3000 N. Rock Road
Newton, KS 67114

Dedication

For Fable and Ava, granddaughters extraordinaire

Preface and Acknowledgments

For readers who know the Uffizi Gallery in Florence intimately, please note: this story takes place sometime before December 2011 during extensive renovations to the museum (see the Afterword for more information). The plan of the building, the order of renovations, the timing of when the Vasari Corridor is open, the characters, and the events in this novel have been modified to suit my story.

No book ever gets written without the help of other writers, beta readers, and the author's family. I am indebted to the Writer's Café (ably let by Frank Chadwick) at the Osher Lifelong Learning Institute at the University of Illinois, and my smaller critique group: fellow authors Julia Kellman, Bev Smith, and Molly MacRae. I am especially grateful to freelance editor Rebecca Bigelow, who did a "cold read" of the manuscript at a crucial phase: she caught many errors and made great suggestions.

To my family, my husband Charlie and our two pampered felines, Truffles and Tesla, I am eternally grateful for your encouragement and your tolerance of burnt dinners and late servings of cat food.

—*Sarah Wisseman, January 2019*

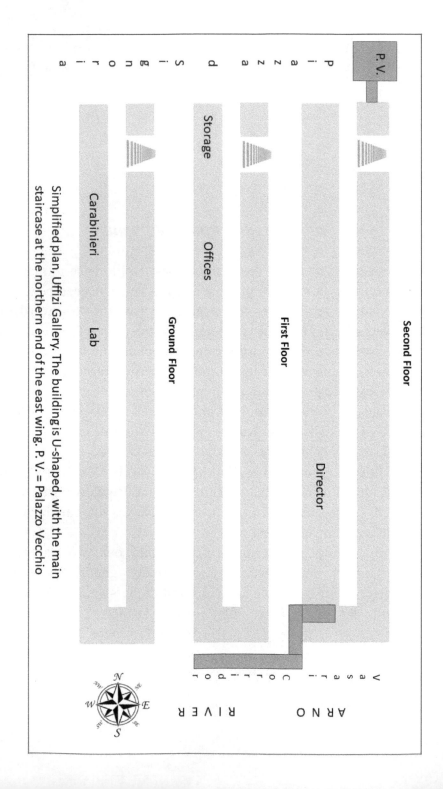

Second Floor

P. V.

First Floor

Director

Ground Floor

Piazza degli Uffizi

Storage

Offices

Carabinieri Lab

vasari corridor

Corridoio

ARNO RIVER

N
NE
E
SE
S
SW
W
NW

Simplified plan, Uffizi Gallery. The building is U-shaped, with the main staircase at the northern end of the east wing. P. V. = Palazzo Vecchio

One

One false paint stroke and she'd be out of a job permanently.

Her hand shook as she picked up her tool—not a brush but a cotton swab—and held it over one of the most famous paintings in the world: Sandro Botticelli's *Birth of Venus*.

Gorgeous. Old. Priceless.

What if she screwed up? This was the most delicate conservation job she'd ever attempted. Could she do it?

Calm down, Flora. You've had excellent training in painting conservation.

But a two-week intensive course in tempera techniques didn't put her in the same class as a painter or conservator who'd spent years working in the medium. She felt as if someone had shoved her into the Olympics before she'd won even a local competition. Could she match the surrounding colors on Venus' left knee exactly, so no viewer could detect the repair? That job paled compared to the excruciating task of cleaning the entire painting without removing any of the original egg-based tempera.

The shouts of construction workers and the revving of a motorcycle outside could not distract her. What a painting! Tastefully nude, marble-white Venus perched on a scallop shell, about to touch the shore. A handmaiden standing ready to cover the goddess with a stunning orange robe. Sky and sea in calming blues and whites, luscious green vegetation, delicate pink roses falling on Venus. Exquisitely rendered bodies, with the flesh of the Wind glowing gold among swirling drapery.

Too bad Flora couldn't kill the tourist who'd thrown his heavy briefcase at the painting. The cell phone had only cracked the protective glass, but the incident had freaked out the chief conservator and accelerated the time table for restoration. All the Botticellis, as well as the masterpieces by Pollaiolo, were being painstakingly cleaned and restored while their new rooms, with state-of-the-art security systems, were readied. Flora had joined dozens of men and women, all laboring in different ways to bring Florence's Uffizi Gallery into the 21st century.

Staring at the painting wasn't getting the job done. She hunched her shoulders up and down to relax them.

C'mon, take a deep breath now.

First, she had to test sections of the painting with different solvents to find the right one to remove grime without disturbing the underlying egg tempera. Small jars of distilled water, liquid soap, and acetone stood close at hand. The acetone was a last resort; she hadn't detected any varnish on the painting with her magnifying visor. She smiled as she remembered a colleague saying he'd used saliva because the enzymes in it removed grime from tempera without harming the painting. Even if she saved up for a week, Flora couldn't produce enough spit to clean a painting this huge.

Using a magnifying visor, she began with water mixed with a tiny bit of mild soap. A little dirt came off, but Flora expected to lift a tiny amount of paint as well. Nothing happened. She added a little more soap and rubbed fractionally harder. Again, nothing. Was there a light varnish over the tempera? Okay, apply a little acetone, in a tiny spot near the edge that would be hidden by the frame once it was replaced.

Bingo. The grime began to lift, but some areas needed acetone while others did fine with soapy water. Flora worked steadily through a mountain of cotton swabs, trying to ignore the loud voices, clanks of ladders, and the screams of drills just on the other side of the wall. Oh, the joys of working in a permanent construction zone! But Flora had no choice. Her body and talents were on loan to the Uffizi as long as Ottavia, her Roman boss, and Giulia, her temporary Florentine boss, deemed necessary.

Wait a minute, that swatch of dark green was turning bright green! Surely the original color had never been that light. She reached into her satchel and pulled out the test cards her class had made for early Renaissance tempera pigments: malachite, verdigris (copper green), ultramarine, cinnabar, red, white, and yellow lead, red lake, and carbon black. They'd mixed their own tempera with ground pigments and an egg yolk-water mixture and then compared the fresh paints with the faded and pitted colors of Old Master paintings.

Look at the workshop notes: *copper green turns brown over time*. Shit.

Flora stared at the Botticelli. Browned green should lighten a little bit with cleaning, but not change hue altogether. The new color resembled early spring redbud leaves in Illinois, where Flora had grown up.

A trickle of unease slid down her spine.

"*Ragazza stupida*! You should have spent more time examining the entire surface before you started cleaning," she muttered as she adjusted her visor and turned her desk lamp so it hit the painting at a raking angle.

After fifteen minutes, she took off her visor, frowning at the painting. It was extraordinarily well preserved for something painted over five centuries earlier. True, there were little nicks in the surface, and darkened pigments, especially the whites.

Flora consulted the notes in the conservation file. The *Birth of Venus* had been cleaned two years earlier by an employee who was no longer at the Uffizi.

Damn—there were no treatment details. A hasty conservator who didn't bother to record anything? No wonder she didn't last.

She examined the painting's surface again. Where were the abrasions caused by that earlier cleaning? Most cleaning left some traces.

Flora fumbled in her drawer for her second, more elaborate visor, the one with miniature microscopes like those used by dentists. She turned to a higher power on each lens. This time she looked at the quality of the paint. Botticelli had pioneered a new medium: *tempera grassa*, or egg yolk made more transparent by adding oil. His paintings gleamed, but this one seemed a bit dull.

She moved on. Botticelli was famous for his delicately blended brush strokes. He built up almost invisible gradations of color, especially in the flesh tones of his human subjects. The total effect was a luminous, complex skin of paint.

Not here. The edges of each stroke stood out, and color changes were clearly apparent, as if an assistant had subbed for the master while he was out to lunch. She reached into her satchel again and compared what she saw with micrographs from her favorite book on Botticelli. A neon sign pulsed in her brain: "Alert! Alert!"

Her heart pounded as her suspicions grew. Cold sweat ran down her sides under her blouse. Flora examined the edges of the huge unframed canvas.

The painter had experimented with color mixtures on the portions of canvas usually hidden by the frame. Here, the colors matched those on the front of the painting, but they were brighter.

She added it up: A coating that didn't behave like a varnish.

A green pigment that changed hue unnaturally, as if it had been painted over with something else.

Brush strokes applied unevenly, without the delicate finesse of Botticelli but still extraordinarily skillful.

Trial color swatches in brighter paint on the edge of the canvas.

She looked at the edges of the canvas again. At one corner, she spied a little circle. Zooming closer with her magnifying glasses, she saw a little face, a smiley face.

It was painted in colors that didn't match anything in the painting.

Flora leaned back in her chair, her thought process in rags.

That little face...modern pigments...almost like "ha, ha" in a cartoon...Who? How? When had it been done?

Her chair legs slammed down onto the stone floor. At this unlucky moment, head conservator Giulia Rossi entered the lab. "Flora! How's it going? I hope you've made progress. We have such an unbelievable amount of work now that the Director—"

She moved close enough to see Flora's face. "What's wrong? Are you okay?"

Flora stood on wobbly knees. She sucked in a deep breath.

"I have good news and bad news for you, Giulia. The good news is...we can stop cleaning this painting. The bad news is...it's not a Botticelli."

Two

"What on earth do you mean? Of course, it's a Botticelli! It's one of the most important works of Renaissance art in all of Italy!" Giulia Rossi's brown eyes snapped as she thumped her notebook on the worktable.

Flora felt her knees wobble again as she confronted the stylish woman twenty years her senior. She inhaled another breath. "I think not. I mean, the original painting is everything you say it is, but *this* painting was not painted in the fifteenth century."

"How could you make such a determination? Are you an expert in art forgery? And that tempera course you just took, it was only two weeks long!"

Anger turned to acid in Flora's stomach. "Giulia, I told you when Ottavia sent me here that my expertise is not on the same level as someone who does tempera exclusively. But the workshop was led by someone who *is* such an expert: the specialist from the Hermitage Museum in St. Petersburg.

"I'm over ninety percent sure this painting's a clever forgery. You don't think I'd make such a statement without proof, do you? Listen…" Speaking with all the authority she could muster, she told Giulia her reasons.

"Show me." Giulia's body quivered inside its expensive sheath of layered black, adorned with a scarf in muted blues and browns.

Flora pointed out the areas where she'd been working. "I think more than one coating was used on this painting. And the pigments on the edge of the canvas don't match the colors on the painting's surface. And look at this little smiley face. I think it's a deliberate taunt by the forger. It couldn't be seen until the frame was removed."

Giulia's shoulders slumped. "*Oddio*, you could be right. We'll have to test the pigments and the surface coating."

"In multiple places. I've only checked four sections of the painting so far."

"I can't believe it." Giulia pulled out a chair and sank into it. "Testing will take at least a day, longer if we have to send the samples to another lab in another city. How on earth…wait. Before I go to the director, we have to figure out when this forgery—and the switch with the original painting—could have happened."

"The painting was last cleaned two years ago. By the way, the conservator who performed that cleaning left no notes—"

"That's not our standard practice, not at all!" exclaimed Giulia. "I knew that conservator was always late, always full of excuses, but not that she left us no documentation!" She shook her sleek bob vigorously.

"Anyhow, I'm guessing the *Venus* hasn't had the glass removed since that cleaning, and it's impossible to thoroughly examine the surface without doing that."

Giulia frowned. "Unless a visiting expert requested a closer examination. I'll check on that. So, if the painting were switched sometime within the last two years—"

"Then the police will have a heck of a time figuring out how and when it was done. And who!" Flora shook her head. "I'd sure like to meet the forger—he's an extraordinary painter."

"Not to mention the multi-million-euro question: *where is the original Botticelli?*"

The two women stared at each other, all previous animosity

forgotten. Then Giulia said, "Last week you told me you have a friend in the Carabinieri's Art Squad in Rome. What's his name?"

"Vittorio Bernini. He's a captain now, and this kind of investigation is right up his alley. And he has great contacts in the art world as well as in our various police forces."

"Here, write down his contact information." Giulia opened her notebook to a blank page and shoved it across the table to Flora.

Flora wrote and closed the notebook, handing it back to her boss.

Giulia stood, patting her hair back into place and squaring her shoulders. "I'm dreading Dr. Romano's reaction. He likes to yell at any employee bearing bad news." Then she brightened. "But he won't waste too much energy on me if the Uffizi Gallery really has been duped by a forger and lost a priceless painting. He'll be too busy explaining this fiasco to the police, the Ministry of Culture, and the press."

Flora stared out the window. She could almost see the vultures of blame gathering in the clouds above the long courtyard between the wings of the museum.

This could be the worst shit storm to ever hit the Uffizi.

Three

It was the day after the discovery of the false Botticelli. As Flora walked to work from her neighborhood south of the Arno River, she indulged in her favorite pastime: daydreaming. When she wasn't thinking about conservation or art forgery, she liked to imagine personalities for the buildings where she worked. The Uffizi Gallery was a perfect candidate, hundreds of years old but as elegant as a duchess dressed in old-fashioned finery...

The Uffizi huddled against the April rain, long arms wrapped around herself for warmth. She sighed, remembering the days when she was a brand-new palazzo in 1560. Then she had been part of the nobility, garbed in gilded cornices, curlicues, pediments, and pilasters, bejeweled with paintings and statues. Important people had traversed her gorgeous spaces planned by Giorgio Vasari for the Grand Duke of Tuscany. Here was her red-walled and gilded Tribune Room, her Niobe Room with the spectacular coffered ceiling, her elegant tapestry-covered long hallways Suitable spaces for the all-powerful Medici family to gather and make important decisions about the future of the city.

Eventually, officious government morons had decided that her rooms should be offices, uffizi, to house their archives. Minions arrived with boxes of ledgers, files, and correspondence. All moldering now, decaying in dusty cabinets and corners.

Water trickled over her pediments and gutters, into ancient cracks between cornice and wall, gathering in pools in forgotten closets. She sighed again. Perhaps she'd turn over despite protesting plaster and creaky timbers. Instead, she stretched a little, smiling as the snaps and pops startled the tourists inside.

The old duchess' breathing calmed as she dreamed of warm sunshine on her skin and limbs. The awake part of her mind plotted how to foil all those contractors, so busy in her bowels. She hugged the secrets of her labyrinthine spread closer, wreathing everything in dust motes and shadows...

This pleasant fantasy lasted Flora the length of her wet journey from her apartment to the staff entrance of the museum.

As she discarded her dripping raincoat and carryall in the current lab on the ground floor, she couldn't help thinking that the Uffizi was not always a duchess. Today, she looked like an old woman caught still in her nightgown when the doorbell rang. The gracious, high-ceilinged hallways were littered with gawking tourists who ignored the palace setting while jostling each other for photographs of every painting and statue. Roped-off rooms revealed untidy tarps and ladders, open toolboxes and lunch wrappers, strewn by careless workmen who shouted and banged around in a ceaseless roar.

Flora fancied she could hear the old woman huffing and grumbling through her dank walls. *Leave me alone, let me return to my glory days, and send all those damned foreigners away!*

Flora stepped over a paint container and a filthy bundled-up tarp, ducked under a ladder blocking the narrow door, and passed into a still older section of the palace.

The L-shaped building was a nightmare to navigate. Flora had to walk completely around the southern end of the ground floor to reach the Grand Staircase—the stairs going up two flights—to the second floor, the museum's major exhibition space. She knew of two other stairs, narrow ones linking only two of the three floors, but these were often roped off or taken over by construction workers.

When Romano had become director two years earlier, he eschewed his predecessor's space in the first floor office area for new digs carved out of a former small gallery on the second floor so he could have more light. This move was only possible because new galleries were being created on the first floor as part of the renovation.

Flora crossed through the Director's Suite to the conference room, a small but elegant space with a painted ceiling and gilded plaster scroll-work around the windows. Most of her new colleagues were already seated, drumming their fingers on the table, or hiding behind their cell phones. Flora chose a chair at the far end of the oval table, noting the contrasting facial expressions: Giulia's grim determination, Alessandro's skepticism—his usual facial cast—and Chiara's smug confidence. Flora's own shock about the forgery had subsided into a feeling that she was being shaken around like towels in a dryer, not knowing which direction was up.

Dr. Stefano Romano, the director, was a handsome but bulky man in an elegant gray suit. Pushing his iron-gray curls back with one hand, he called the meeting to order. "We are here to discuss how to proceed after hearing *Signorina* Garibaldi's theory that our Botticelli's *Birth of Venus* is not all it should be." He pinned Flora with a cold gaze and said flatly, "No one could do this. There isn't a painter alive who could do a forgery this skilled."

"There are skilled forgers in every major city in Europe—in the world—who could forge even such a masterpiece as the *Birth of Venus* or *La Primavera*," Flora replied.

"I agree." Chiara Altavilla, curator of medieval art, thrust her jaw forward. "Anyone who has seriously studied painting has encountered gifted copiers, artists who can render exactly what a master has done." She sniffed. "And remember, a copy is not a forgery until the painter tries to pass it off as an original."

Romano quelled the speakers with a glare. He nodded to Flora. "Tell us, please, exactly what you *think* you found."

Dismally, Flora registered the antagonism in his manner. All eyes turned her way, making her feel small and exposed.

Give it your best shot and tell your truth.

Flora started slowly, striving to explain everything in sequence as it had happened. She described her process of trying different solvents and the incremental steps she'd taken, leading to her dismaying conclusion that the *Birth of Venus* was an expert copy. She realized as she spoke that the painter hadn't signed it "S. Botticelli," so his work only became a forgery when someone hung it in the place of the original to confound both experts and tourists.

"I don't believe it!" Alessandro sneered. "How could this be? How could Miss Garibaldi, a visiting scholar, notice these things when we conservators did not? What is your training, your expertise to do this?" He sat back in his chair, pleased with his performance.

"Enough, Alessandro." Director Romano glanced down at his notes. "*Signora* Rossi informs me that Flora is a professional conservator. She is well-trained in art history and conservation techniques and has recently completed a special course in the treatment of tempera paintings. This is correct, *Signorina*?"

Flora nodded. "Yes. I should add that my special subject at university was painting of the Renaissance. Also, the recent course gave me hands-on experience working with tempera paints. We made paint mixtures from different recipes and artists and observed how each mixture behaved under different conditions: moist, dry, hot, and cold. The only factor we couldn't simulate was time, because we only had weeks instead of centuries."

Chiara spoke up. "Very commendable. But some of your early training was in America, right? American conservators are not as good as Italian ones." She tossed her long black hair.

No ally there, thought Flora. *I could dispute her statement, but why bother?*

Giulia came to Flora's defense. "When I checked Flora's vita before she was hired, I saw she trained at Winterthur and New York

University. Those programs are up to our standards. And she tells me her recent course was taught by an expert from the Laboratory for Tempera Conservation at the Hermitage Museum in the former Soviet Union."

"Okay, okay. So where are we with the testing of this painting?" Romano turned to Giulia.

"I have the pigment test results right here. We were lucky: our Uffizi chemists did a rush job for us."

The director took the paper from Giulia and read the contents quickly.

He swallowed, his Adam's apple jumping and his mouth working as if something tasted horrid. "I still cannot believe this. Several of the pigments, such as the white, have modern compositions: the white contains zinc or titanium instead of lead."

Chiara slumped in her chair. Alessandro's jaw dropped.

Flora knew zinc white pigment wasn't invented until the nineteenth century and the first use of titanium white dated to the twentieth century. "How about the green pigment? That was the color that looked really strange to me."

Romano grimaced. "Chromium green. First use, nineteenth century."

Flora's heart beat faster. The director might make terrible faces, but he agreed with her. As horrible as it was that the Botticelli was a forgery, he supported her judgment!

The director's face brightened. "Of course, the painting could still be an original touched up in modern times."

"No, it could not," said a tall, skinny man with rumpled brown hair who had just entered the room. "I have examined the brush strokes with my special lenses and microscope attachment, and they are *not* Botticelli's. I'd go further and say no student of Botticelli did this work, either. Much as you hate to admit it, *Dottore* Romano, we have a forgery on our hands. That means a major scandal when it hits the press and social media." Federico Armani, curator of Renaissance Art, drew out a chair with a screech and flung himself into it. His brown eyes scanned the faces around him, daring defiance.

The room exploded with questions.

"*Oddio!* Who did it? Who had access to that painting?"

"When was the forgery swapped for the original? I can't believe that—"

"Where is the original now?"

"Have the police been notified? How about the Art Squad in Rome?"

The last question upset the director. He slammed his fist on the table. "I decide when the police are called in! And take note: this news will *not* reach the press, understood? Not until we have complete answers to some of these questions." Romano let his stern gaze rest on each face in turn. "Anyone caught leaking information outside this room will be fired."

An uncomfortable silence descended while they all avoided looking at each other.

Flora was pretty sure Romano was violating the law by not calling the police immediately, given the magnitude of the theft. She dared to speak again: "*Dottore*, I checked the conservation records, and the painting was cleaned two years ago. That provides a possible window of time for the swap of the original with the forgery."

Armani said, "You are assuming that conservator was experienced enough to detect a forgery while cleaning a painting."

Good point, thought Flora.

"She was not very experienced—and she documented nothing," said Giulia. She turned to the boss. "*Dottore*, how can we find all these answers without help from the outside? At some point, the TPC—the Art Squad—of the Carabinieri must know about the theft and—"

"I will make the decision when we inform the *Tutela Patrimonio Culturale!*" thundered Romano.

Giulia clammed up and slid her shaking hands under the table.

Romano leaned back in his chair and closed his eyes for a long moment. When he opened them, his voice had softened. "What we do is this: we gather all the internal evidence we can find: who has had access to that painting for any reason and when during this eternal hell of construction the painting might have been lifted. Then I will call the Carabinieri and I will do everything in my power to keep their investigation out of the public eye."

Easier said than done. Flora stared out the window, struggling to keep her face unreadable as the director doled out tasks to everyone except Flora, the visiting pariah who'd upset everything.

She doubted the director would find nearly as much information as he wanted. Most museums were better at describing their artifacts than keeping track of what their employees did. Here at the Uffizi, paintings and statues took precedence over live people.

And keeping something this explosive away from the ever-hungry press?

Good luck with that, Dottore.

Four

Flora left Giulia behind in the conference room, conferring with Romano. She could feel the sweat under her tunic top cooling after the tension of the meeting. As she passed the multipaned windows and major galleries of the Uffizi's top floor, the gears in her mind meshed and ideas flowed.

A two-year window for the biggest crime the Uffizi had ever faced—this is what she needed to convey to Vittorio Bernini. She descended the crowded Grand Staircase—the same one the tourists used—wishing the new third staircase under construction halfway down the west wing was open.

The biggest problem the Carabinieri faced was that this Renaissance palace had been under continuous renovation since right after World War II. The visionaries of Florence had decided to expand the available galleries in such a way that the museum would never close to the money-paying public. To make this happen, art collections switched places like dance partners, one or two rooms at a time. Except for breaks caused by the catastrophic Florentine flood of 1966 and a Mafia bombing near the museum's entrance in 1993, the expansion galloped ahead into the twenty-first century with rotating crews.

Flora felt some pity for the museum staff stuck with working in a construction zone for the foreseeable future. She, however, would high-tail it back to Rome as soon as she completed her current projects.

During her year-long romance with Vittorio, Flora had experienced several opportunities to assist the Carabinieri and the Art Squad with her inside knowledge of conservation practices and art history. She enjoyed arguing with Vittorio when he shared aspects of his cases and invited her opinions. He frequently violated his department's rule of no communication with civilians because he knew she could keep her mouth shut. Unfortunately for Vittorio, Flora sometimes put herself in danger by chasing down clues without telling him where she was going. She smiled ruefully as she remembered being chased through the catacombs of Rome and being hunted in a museum in Bolzano. Served her right for being so impulsive.

As Flora descended two flights of stairs to the ground floor and walked around the southern end of the palace to the lab, she started a mental list of questions about access to the Botticelli painting. Had anyone besides the conservator who couldn't be bothered taking notes removed the *Birth of Venus* for any reason during that two - year window? If they had, did anyone record the episode? Were there occasions when the protective glass was removed, but the painting left in place? The only reason she could think of for such a maneuver would be if art historians or scientists had come to examine the painting with instruments and special lighting. Experts were often called in for evaluations of brushstrokes, surface treatment, underpainting, or pigment analysis for different technical studies— and forgery detection. Any such event should be recorded somewhere, since removing the glass and allowing experts to work would require permission and staff assistance.

Arriving at her station in the conservation lab, Flora sat in her chair and grabbed her coffee mug. She pulled out her notebook to scribble a few notes to herself.

The other big question is how soon she should tell Vittorio? *Dottore* Romano would be furious no matter when she did it, because he'd see it as gross interference. But Flora knew her conscience wouldn't let her rest until she had made that phone call. The switch of a world-famous painting with a forgery was indisputably Art Squad business.

Five

Giulia left the staff meeting with her boss. Her hands still shook slightly as she walked with him back to his office, only a few steps away from the second floor conference room. His physical presence, so close to her in the narrow hallway, caused her skin to tingle and her breath to catch in her throat.

"I hope that young woman is not going to cause more trouble," Romano said. "I don't need any more surprises this week."

"Stefano, I know that Flora's a good, conscientious worker. With her background, she could not have stayed quiet about the false Botticelli."

He unlocked his door. "No, I suppose not. I just can't believe it. We were so—I mean, our museum has better security than most Italian museums. I don't see how anyone could have spirited a painting, especially one so large, out of the gallery."

Giulia wondered if the painting was really outside the museum. What if someone had hidden it, just until a sale could be arranged? No, didn't make sense; anyone wanting to steal such a famous painting would have a buyer lined up for immediate delivery and payment. Stealing it and storing it was too dangerous. She took her usual chair opposite Romano, waiting for him to settle down after smoothing his hair, unbuttoning his suit jacket and lighting a cigarette.

So much for the law restricting smoking inside public places. He probably figured the boss could do whatever he pleased in his private office and none of his staff would report him.

Inhaling a big, restoring lungful of smoke, Romano fastened his gaze on her face. "Giulia, this is going to be a god-awful scandal when it breaks. I want you to help me deal with the media."

"Of course, boss. I'll start drafting a press release." She shivered a little, relishing having his attention focused on her, relieved that he still wanted her to help him cope with difficult situations. His sudden smile went right to her gut, warming her insides. His teeth gleamed white, despite his nicotine habit, and his hands were surprisingly shapely for such a big man. *Dio mio*, she thought. I'm falling in love with my boss. The absolute stupidest thing I could do, especially since his wife Adona is my cousin. But when did love ever pay attention to reason?

"Don't prepare more than the background on Botticelli and why this work is so significant. We don't know yet how the Carabinieri will want to present this case to the public, or how much they'll want to say."

"I understand. I suppose the obvious question is, when did it happen?"

He snorted. "Any time during the past six months, I reckon."

Giulia looked at her boss. "Or longer, if nothing happened since the last cleaning of the *Birth of Venus*. Do you know how many times the alarm system has been turned off since the workmen started on the new staircase and the restrooms? I don't. It would be easy to move in and out of the museum during one of our busy times—"

"Not with a huge painting under your arm!" snapped Romano.

"I wonder how hard it would be to take it out of the frame? I mean—"

"Spare me your speculations, Giulia. I think it's time you got back to work."

Uh oh. Better leave before I get my head snapped off.

Giulia hid the irrational feeling of hurt at her dismissal and nodded. "See you later, then. I'm going to make a list of times when the Botticelli has been out of its frame for cleaning or touch-up."

"Do that." He picked up the phone and spun his chair toward the window.

Six

Flora called Vittorio that evening, as soon as she was reasonably sure he'd be off duty.

"What's wrong, *cara*? You'd don't sound like yourself at all."

"You're right. Everything's awful. I don't know what to do. And I wish you were here." Flora's longing sped through the ether between Florence and Rome.

She could hear Vittorio Bernini's chuckle perfectly, as if he were in the same room.

"I'd prefer you said you wanted me there first."

Flora clutched her cell in one hand and her wine glass in the other, pacing the sitting room of her Airbnb apartment. "You know what I mean. The thing is…we've had a theft of a major painting. I mean, a substitution. Actually both: A theft of the original and a substitution that's an expert copy. A forgery. And we don't know how long ago it was done."

"A forgery? Are you sure? Maybe you're finding drama where there is none."

Flora's irritation rose; this was no time for Vittorio's brand of teasing. "There is no fake drama, this is real! And it's not just my assessment—we've had the pigments tested."

"I'm sorry. I should not have cast doubt on your work."

Damn straight. You should keep your trap shut sometimes.

"Thanks for the apology, Vittorio. But I wish you'd choose

another way to get my goat. Hasn't Giulia called you?"

His tone sharpened. "No one has called. Giulia is your boss, correct? What about the museum boss, *Dottore* Romano? Surely he should call us."

"He's prickly. He wants to investigate first and then call you." Flora could almost see Vittorio shaking his head.

"Your director is flouting the law. *Cara*, you must tell me everything. This is Art Squad business."

Flora clutched the cell phone tighter in her hand. "I agree. But if I tell you everything and the director finds out who called the Carabinieri behind his back, he'll have my head. He wants to get all his ducks in a row before he calls you people in."

"'Ducks in a row?' Oh, I get it. Another one of your crazy American expressions. Listen, Flora. Museum directors don't know much about police procedure. And hordes of museum staff tramping all over the place will destroy any physical evidence there is. *Cara*, you must tell me, *immediatamente*. I will see you don't get fired."

Feeling her shoulders sag with relief, Flora told him everything.

Vittorio asked several pertinent questions and then was silent.

"How would it be if I arrive suddenly as part of an official inspection tour? We're due to visit the Uffizi next month…I could just pretend to move the trip forward to a day or two from now. Don't say a word in advance. That way, I'll be there to shield you from the director's wrath if he suspects the real reason we came."

"I love it. Just come as soon as you can."

Flora ended the call. She wandered over to the tiny porch off the bedroom of the apartment, gazing out the double glass door at other people's laundry hung on retractable clotheslines across a grubby inner courtyard. Beyond the neighboring building, she could see the tall, skinny cypress trees gracing the Boboli Gardens.

Time for another glass of wine and a little supper.

And sleep? Fat chance. She had far too much to think about for sleep.

Seven

Flora slept badly, waking several times during the night to find her covers tumbled and her nightgown sweaty. When the alarm sounded, she jerked out of an uneasy dream in which she'd been tiptoeing through the Uffizi in the dark, hunting for a forger who painted pseudo-masterpieces while guards slept at their stations.

She took a hot shower and inhaled two cups of espresso with sugar, hoping to kick-start her brain into workaday mode. She spent more time than usual at the mirror, rubbing concealer under her eyes and wielding an eye pencil and mascara to create the impression of a wide-awake, reliable museum professional in control of her emotions.

Liar, she told herself as she viewed the result. The thin worried face, tired brown eyes, and cloud of curly dark hair were not convincing. She looked like someone who'd sat up all night in a crowded train station.

Flora gathered up satchel, keys, cell phone, and coat and left the tiny apartment. Stairs led down to street level, and she popped out on Via dei Serragli near the Palazzo Pitti on the south side of the Arno. A cold, insinuating wind greeted her, whipping her open jacket against her torso. Droplets of rain fell off a straggly tree near the entrance, making Flora raise her hood and curse.

April in Florence. Wet, chilly, and distinctly unfriendly. Granted, Rome wasn't much better this time of year, but at least it was home. She missed the larger apartment she shared with Vittorio in Trastevere, the familiar dishes and small objects she'd collected from her student years, and *Gattino*, "little cat." Gattino was the wayward cat they'd acquired as a kitten and never gotten around to re-naming.

Flora took the most direct route, turning right on the Via dei Serumido to cut over to the Via Romana and the Ponte Vecchio. She passed cafes (open) and pizzerias (still shuttered) and nipped into her favorite café near the bridge for a pastry and a third coffee to go.

The Ponte Vecchio, normally crowded with artisans and tourists in the summer, stood sullenly in the rain. Jewelry shops, upscale boutiques, all closed so early in the morning. Flora glanced up at the smooth walls of pale pink and cream stucco above her eye level. Occasional windows punctuated the surface, but they looked too regularly spaced to be apartments. Making a mental note to return on the other side of the medieval bridge so she could gawk at the gold and orange buildings with green shutters, she turned into the Uffizi *loggia* and nearly collided with a thin man in a suit.

"Vittorio! You aren't supposed to be here yet!" she cried.

He pulled her behind a construction barrier and held her arms to keep her from jumping up and down. "I wanted to surprise you. Looks like I succeeded. I also wanted to tell you we must hide our personal relationship as long as possible. *Va bene?*"

"*Certo*. But Giulia already knows you are my friend—I didn't tell her we live together in Rome—so Dr. Romano may have heard something."

He nodded. "All right, I'll play it by ear. Sometimes you learn more about people when they're upset, and if he knows you have called the Carabinieri, he'll be pissed."

Oh, yes, he will be. And he's the sort of boss who retaliates.

"Guess what? I brought Gattino. If you give me a key, I'll send our driver to your apartment with the cat."

"Fantastic. I've missed him so much."

"As much as you missed me?" he teased.

"More. You know that cat is the most important member of our household."

He laughed.

Flora gave Vittorio a quick goodbye kiss and left him to make his official entrance with his colleague through the main gate. She ducked in the staff door. Inside, she showed her badge to security and took the long corridor around to the lab, her heart accelerating as she thought of the confrontations on the horizon.

Their current lab was a converted storage area with very little natural light. Giulia and the other conservators longed for the day when they could move into the new lab, under construction in the east wing of the first floor above them. Flora had just enough time to don her work smock and lay out her tools before Giulia summoned her by cell phone.

"Staff meeting, upstairs, on the double. The Carabinieri are here."

"They are? Okay, on my way," said Flora. She grabbed her notebook and took the stairs two at a time.

Entering the conference room, she spied Vittorio immediately, standing in a huddle with Giulia and Dr. Romano. Vittorio raised one eyebrow slightly but gave no other sign that he knew her.

"*Signorina* Garibaldi!" Dr. Romano announced her with a scowl. "*Capitano* Bernini says he knows you."

Uh oh. The beans had been spilled already, and the director was not happy.

"Yes." Not knowing how much Vittorio had revealed, she kept her mouth shut.

"We met at a conference on art conservation," Vittorio said dismissively. "But I had no idea she was in Florence."

Flora glanced at Giulia to judge her reaction. Giulia's brow furrowed; was she wondering how Vittorio happened to be here so quickly after Flora had given Giulia his contact information?

He turned back to Romano. *"Dottore,* we were in the area and stopped by to see if any problems have cropped up at the museum in the past nine months."

Oh really, thought Flora. If that explanation sounded thin to her, it probably did to the other staff. She turned her gaze on her boss.

The look on Dr. Romano's face could have curdled milk. He took Bernini aside and talked for several minutes as other museum staff gathered around the table. Finally, Dr. Romano gestured for everyone to sit, and a sandy-haired colleague of Bernini's sat to the director's left, laptop at the ready.

Romano took a deep breath. "Events have overtaken us, and the theft of the Botticelli is now in the hands of the Art Squad. This is *Capitano* Vittorio Bernini, and his colleague is *Tenente* Raffael Esposito. *Capitano,* I turn the meeting over to you." He sat back in his chair with shoulders bunched with tension.

Vittorio's gaze swept the assembled staff. "Esposito and I represent the Art Squad in Rome, but we'll be working with the local Florentine Carabinieri and *Polizia di Stato.* Each of you will be interviewed later, but what I need now is information on the Botticelli painting that has been replaced by a forgery. Specifically, have any of you noticed unusual interest in the painting over the past several weeks?"

No one said anything for a moment. Then Alessandro said, "The problem is, the staff are hardly ever in the Botticelli gallery except to pass through on the way to somewhere else. And it's too easy to take the wide main corridor and miss the galleries altogether, if you're in a hurry."

Chiara added. "We're all wrapped up in our work, most of which is on a rush schedule to keep pace with the gallery renovations. And the continuous construction takes up any extra attention we have— the noisy interruptions are a constant irritant."

Flora nodded her agreement, remembering with longing the spacious and quiet laboratory where she worked in Rome. Then, she remembered something. "Captain Bernini, the current Botticelli gallery is temporary; all the paintings were moved recently so the regular Botticelli rooms could have their electricity and air-conditioning upgraded."

He nodded. "That's useful information. Anyone know how long ago the paintings were moved?"

Giulia said, "I think about nine months ago."

Vittorio said, "Do you have a list of when the Botticelli has been unprotected, meaning when the glass was removed for examination?"

Dr. Romano raised one eyebrow at Giulia Rossi, who turned pink.

"I thought we did," she said warily. "But I can't lay my hands on it."

"Special visitors, such as art experts, should be tracked by the head guard at the entrance of the museum," Alessandro said. "He has a roster."

Carabiniere Esposito asked, "What about the construction schedule? Surely there is a record of when the alarm system has been turned off?"

The museum director spread his hands. "That happens several times per week because of the ongoing construction. I would be very surprised if someone had written down date and time every time. Perhaps the electrician knows."

Vittorio jotted down a couple of notes and closed his notebook. "We will take a tour of the construction zone, and then I would like to meet the head of construction and the electrician."

"Certainly," said Dr. Romano. He glanced around the room. "The rest of you can get back to work."

Flora stood, watching Vittorio's face.

He wore a scowl and his eyebrows formed a straight line across the top of his nose. He didn't look happy.

Eight

Vittorio Bernini was definitely not happy. In fact, he had a sinking feeling in his lower gut that this job would be the most complicated and frustrating of his career.

He and Esposito followed Director Romano to the north end of the first floor of the Uffizi, where a new gallery was being carved out of a storeroom, formerly the site of mountains of files from the State Archives of Florence.

Romano explained how the Uffizi was gradually reclaiming parts of this floor for new offices, a new state-of-the-art conservation lab, and compact storage—a system of shelves that slid together to save space. Other new spaces in the works included new galleries so more of the museum's collections could be on display instead of in storage, and more space for temporary exhibitions. "As I'm sure you know, exhibition space is at a premium in these older buildings. The most important new space will accommodate our traveling exhibit about looted artwork. It's called 'Stolen Art: Robbing the Homes and Museums of Europe" and will include many artworks taken by the Nazis during World War Two as well as more recent thefts. Many of the looted pieces have been recovered and returned to the families of original owners. Several owners are now sending their returned treasures to us as we speak, because the first venue for the exhibit is the Uffizi."

Bernini nodded. After his recent investigation of looted art caches in the catacombs of Rome, he knew quite a bit about which paintings had been recovered and which were still missing, despite the best efforts of police and art historians from around the world. And he found it extremely interesting that the Uffizi was currently accepting multiple loans from all over Europe. Such comings and goings of people and large crates could provide opportunities for things such as a stolen Botticelli to move out of the Uffizi.

Bernini looked around and noticed two, sometimes three, doors in each room. Were some of them closet doors, or inner storerooms? He asked Romano.

"Yes, you are right. This is a very old building, and it was built with many compartments. We don't even use all the rooms."

Aha, thought Bernini. *Possible hiding places?*

He began to ask questions about keys while Esposito took notes.

~ * ~

An hour later, Bernini took himself out for a coffee after telling Esposito to begin interviewing the staff.

He found a café in the Piazza della Signoria near the museum and ordered an espresso. When it arrived at his sunlit table, Bernini lit a cigarette and stared absently at tourists passing by. Why did he have such a bad feeling about this case? Perhaps because it wasn't a straightforward robbery. Instead, someone had deliberately replaced a priceless painting with a forgery while thumbing his nose at the security system, the museum staff, and everything the Uffizi stood for.

Then there was the building: a sixteenth century monster with multiple levels and an insane number of entrances and exits. An above-ground catacomb, constantly under renovation, with access given to staff, construction workers, tourists, and God knew who else.

His first task: to narrow down when the painting substitution took place.

Second, to determine who had access at that time. Staff? Electricians? Special visitors?

Third, how was the crime committed?

Fourth, *whodunnit*? And was it one person, or a team of people working together?

Unanswerable questions continued to parade through his brain.

As he drained his coffee cup, a chilling thought rose in his consciousness.

The mind behind this theft must be especially adept at complex planning, combined with a malicious intent to deceive as many people as possible for as long as possible.

That rack of questions was quite a load without worrying about Flora.

Vittorio sighed as he took a sip of water. He'd lived through two investigations with Flora—the one where'd they'd met when she began as a suspect in a murder in Siena and ended as a police ally. The second investigation, only a few months ago in the catacombs of Rome, had tested their growing love in so many ways. Near-death had a way of sharpening one's focus.

Now he had to figure out how to use her skills without endangering her life again.

Tricky, since her job required that she be at the crime scene five days per week.

Nine

Supposing I wanted to rob a major museum with a state-of-the art security system...how would I go about it?

Flora's mind jiggled with questions as she roamed the Uffizi Gallery on her lunch hour. Of course, this problem was really Vittorio's, but he had shut down on her after giving her a brief outline of his private meeting with the museum director. Vittorio tended to be grumpy during the first day or two of a major investigation; Flora understood that, and sympathized. He wanted to get it right from the beginning as he navigated complex interactions between the Carabinieri, the *Polizia di Stato*, and informants he'd never worked with before.

Time for her to snoop a little. Vittorio would quickly realize her position on the museum staff gave her valuable insights as well as inside information. Her participation could save the police time, and time was critical in solving art crimes.

Flora paced slowly around the edges of the temporary Botticelli gallery, noting the black security cameras lurking in the upper corners of the room. The guard, in a dark uniform, perched on a folding chair near the entrance. He paid no attention to Flora's glances that touched everything except the famous paintings in the room.

Most paintings were protected by glass; how could anyone get close enough to damage one or steal it? Flora noticed that paintings varied in the degree and type of protection. Some had glass over the painting, inside the frame; some had glass extending over the frame like the *Birth of Venus*; some had no glass at all that she could detect. Instead, at least two of the larger paintings were protected only by a railing, a physical barrier to prevent a viewer from getting too close. Did the choice of protection relate to the value of each painting, the surface treatment (varnish or no varnish, for example), or both? She'd ask the other conservators.

Looking up at the camera just above her head, Flora had a new thought. *Was the security system in place now the same as the one when the Botticelli painting was replaced?* The answer depended on when the event had happened, and so far, neither the museum staff nor the police could pin the time down.

Vittorio made lists of the questions he had to ask and the people to be interviewed for each case. He kept these in a small notebook that was always on his body. Flora sat on a padded bench and pulled out her own notebook.

Cameras and alarms: when were they installed?

Surely, with the amount of gallery renovation taking place over the past two decades, there were times when repairs and replacements had to be made...

Flora entered the next gallery, noting that the guard was chatting with another guard, both blissfully unaware of the light tourist traffic and Flora's presence. She circled this room, stopping in front of a niche in the wall. Why had she never noticed this?

The niche was an inset chamber, three-sided, with fake painted columns framing it. A straight chair squatted inside, with a velvet-covered rope on stanchions in front of it. Not a guard chair, because no guard could sit there without removing the barrier. The paint matched that of the surrounding gallery walls, and the trim around the niche gleamed white and smooth. Too smooth.

Flora stared. That niche had been a doorway once, she was sure of it. What was behind that niche, and why had it been blocked off?

She made a note in her notebook with another question: *how many other rooms have been modified in a similar fashion, and what's behind the niches? Passageways? Extra storage?*

Flora crossed the corridor into the new Botticelli gallery. She was forced to stop just inside the doorway since electricians and plasterers were busy with renovation.

Wait a minute. Not all the walls joined in traditional corners in the room. Instead, some formed free-standing structures.

She asked the guard about the arrangement.

"This is the newest renovation. These walls form what the construction chief calls 'theatrical wings.' They sub-divide the original gallery and provide more space for hanging and viewing paintings."

Flora thanked him and made another note.

She exited the gallery and located a bench in the gilded hallway at the north end of the Uffizi. This space, stuffed with sculptures, connected the two wings of the museum and led to what would be a stunning outdoor café in the next few months.

She gazed out the window at the soaring towers of the Palazzo Vecchio next door and continued the list in her notebook.

BEG, BORROW, OR STEAL:

Building plans of the museum over time: who has them?

Schedule of changes in the security system

Renovation schedule for past ten years

List of conservation projects requiring disarming the security system and removing glass

List of scholars and other special visitors allowed access to the Botticelli.

Flora looked at her list with a cynical eye. What were the chances that all such records—if they existed—had been kept where they could be found? Museum records involving capital expenditures tended to migrate to the tight-fisted hands and dusty file drawers of the Ministry of Culture, never to be seen again.

She smiled. Vittorio and his team would need all the help they could get.

Ten

Vittorio Bernini bagged a table in his favorite Florentine *trattoria* and waited for Flora.

The little restaurant, located just south of the Arno, boasted quiet nooks and comfortable chairs. The family-owned establishment specialized in favorites such as rabbit stew, tripe, and steak prepared in the special Florentine fashion.

He was in the mood for a meaty stew and strong red wine. Perhaps Flora had some encouraging thoughts; he had none. Normally cheerful and optimistic at the start of an investigation, Vittorio felt off-balance and uncertain. He didn't know how much time he had before he had to return to Rome. The Uffizi case promised to be one of the most important and difficult of his career; he wanted to give it his full attention. Maybe he could convince his superiors to reassign his other cases?

Vittorio signaled to the waiter and ordered a red *Brunello di Montalcino*. While sipping slowly, waiting for Flora, he glanced appreciatively around the restaurant. The decorations were simple but effective…straw-wrapped wine bottles, handmade ceramic plates with floral designs, blooming bulbs in attractive pots filled the wide window sills of the dining room, which was sunk a meter below street level.

Flora appeared, dressed in a sky-blue sweater tunic and narrow black pants. Her curls tumbled over her delicate face as she picked her way through diners whose tables and chairs crowded the narrow restaurant.

Vittorio's mood took a turn for the better as he greeted her, and the tension eased in his shoulders. At least he had an ally here. More than that, she was the woman he loved. Experience had taught him that Flora could be impulsive and get herself into trouble, but her quick mind and people skills outweighed this minor defect. Besides, life might get rather dull and predictable if Flora didn't surprise him with her insights, or stick her pretty nose into other people's business.

"Hi," she said as she scooted her chair closer to the table. She peered at his face. "You look tired and frustrated."

"Indeed, I am both those things. But I'm more cheerful now that you're here. Have some wine." He poured her a glass from the bottle.

She took a sip of wine and her eyes widened as she tasted it. "Lovely wine. So, any more details about *Dottore* Romano?"

He weighed his response. With Flora, he'd often bypassed the Art Squad policy to keep investigations completely confidential. He'd tell her just enough about each investigation to keep her in the picture without revealing his sources. This time, however, her job and her future career involved working at the crime scene. She could hardly be asked to recuse herself from an important conservation job set up by her own boss in Rome.

"Uh...Flora, remind me...how much do your colleagues know about our relationship?"

Flora nodded as if she'd anticipated this question. "You asked me that when you arrived. I told Giulia I had a friend on the Art Squad. She remembered that and asked me for your contact info before she went to Dr. Romano. Unless we betrayed ourselves in the staff meeting, no one here knows that we are lovers or that we live together in Rome."

She smiled at him. "I haven't made close friends here. That's hard to do in such a short time."

"Good. That means we can—" A waiter appeared at his elbow and asked what they would have.

"The *gnudi* for me," Flora said, "And the house salad with the balsamic vinegar dressing as my second course."

Vittorio read the description of her choice. "Spinach and ricotta—sounds great. But I'll have the *pasta arrabbiata* and the *bistecca alla fiorentina*."

"Cooked how?" asked the waiter.

"Medium is fine."

The waiter topped up their wine and water glasses and took the menus away with him.

Flora said, "You were saying?"

Vittorio gazed at Flora's eager face and groaned silently to himself. She wouldn't like what he was about to say. "Flora, I think we have to proceed differently on this investigation."

Her eager look was replaced with wariness. "Oh? How do you mean?"

"You are an employee of the museum that is now a crime scene."

"A *temporary* employee. This job wasn't supposed to last longer than a month. I was thinking I would ask Ottavia for an extension. There's plenty more conservation to do, and if I stay, I can be useful to you."

He sighed. "I know. But I've been thinking. Instead of being an official, visible consultant to the Carabinieri, it might be smarter if everyone knew you are my girlfriend."

Flora frowned. "You mean it might be **safer for** me, but not necessarily for you."

"Huh?"

"Remember how our last villain snatched me in the catacombs in order to have leverage over you?"

"I can't forget that, ever."

Flora gave him a straight look. "So, think again. The flip side of this situation is that I'm on the inside, as a member of the museum's staff, and you are not. I can be an extra set of eyes and ears."

Vittorio smiled. "Except when your face betrays you."

She put her glass down with a distinct click. "Arrgh! I'm tired of hearing that my face is like an open window!"

He laughed. "It's one of your most delightful characteristics—but it makes you a lousy spy."

The waiter returned with their pasta dishes. Flora took one forkful and her expression grew dreamy. "This is amazing. The spinach complements the creamy ricotta perfectly. I *might* give you a bite. If I think you deserve it."

Vittorio gave her his most soulful look and moved his fork toward her plate.

"Not so fast," Flora said, pulling her plate with the green pasta away from him. "Okay, I have a transparent face when you're around, but that doesn't mean I can't hide my feelings from people like Romano. I can still be useful to the Carabinieri."

Vittorio placed his glass carefully on the table. "True. But you know already, *cara*, that art theft cases often involve more than one crime. Too much money is involved. I hate having you in the middle of an ugly situation. We've not had a murder yet, but it could happen."

Flora put her fork down and spoke slowly. "Vittorio, we've had this discussion before in Rome—and Siena. Remember? I can gather information for you, about people's habits and connections, in a way that won't put me in danger. If we *don't* admit our relationship, the museum staff will continue to speak freely around me. They won't talk if they know I'm a police stooge, updating you every night."

"That only works as long as Giulia doesn't blab, or no one spots us coming in or out of the same apartment."

Vittorio's steak and Flora's salad arrived. He welcomed the interruption because it gave him time to think. Besides, he was hungry. He carved off two delicious bites of the perfectly cooked meat surrounded by white beans and potatoes.

Flora returned to her pasta without speaking.

The next part of the meal passed in silence while they enjoyed the food.

Vittorio took a long breath, "Flora, I'm sorry. I realize I can be a bit over-protective—"

Her lips relaxed and her eyes stopped resembling dark pools of reproach.

"But sometimes it's so difficult to strike the right balance between using your talents and keeping you safe. Not to mention keeping my job. Now, let's think together how you can help without getting yourself into trouble."

Flora leaned forward. "I have some ideas. And I made a list of observations and questions while I toured the Botticelli rooms—both the temporary ones and the newly renovated ones. Have you noticed the wall niches? They look so odd."

"Yes, I have. They look exactly like former doorways that have been closed off arbitrarily to enclose the galleries. I wonder what's behind them."

"So do I. I bet I could get one of the guards to give me a behind-the-scene tour."

"No, Flora. Leave that to me."

Eleven

Flora left the apartment early after spending the night alone; Vittorio spent his first night in Florence in a hotel provided by the Carabinieri. He planned to move into her rented space that evening.

The weather had improved, producing a watery sunshine and cold but not frigid temperatures. As Flora navigated the almost non-existent sidewalk next to dumpsters and tiny cars parked at right-angles to the other cars lining the street, she replayed an old conversation she'd had with Vittorio back in Siena.

"Why do you love conservation?" he'd asked her.

"Because we're preserving glorious works of art for the future, one piece at a time. To me, it's the direct application of studying art history…keeping the legacy from decaying out of existence."

"I assume you hate forgers," he said.

"Of course. Their work muddies the legacy and confuses the museum-going public. And it makes me angry that so many forgers can't be stopped. One fake is unmasked, but ten others make it onto the art market as authentic pieces and migrate to museum walls or into wealthy collector's private galleries."

Vittorio loved playing devil's advocate. "Do you ever think an expert forgery is in itself a work of art, worthy of admiration?"

She considered this. "No, because to think that way undermines everything museums stand for! I admire technical ability, but no matter how good a forger is, he shouldn't be allowed to profit from other people's ignorance about what is authentic and what isn't. And Vittorio, isn't it odd to be talking this way when your job is to recover stolen art—original art?"

"I just love art. All competent art, no matter who made it."

"But if a masterpiece is found to be a fake, shouldn't it be removed from public view?"

Flora smiled ruefully as she recalled this ongoing debate. It cut to the heart of her chosen profession: restoring masterpieces and using her knowledge of materials and techniques to detect forgeries. Did she want to do this kind of work forever? There were times when sitting at her table got a little boring. Would such work mesh with having children? Probably, but she wasn't even sure she wanted children, at least not yet.

Flora said hello to a stray cat, a stripy fellow with a torn ear. He ignored her, intent on finding breakfast under parked cars. All Italian cats knew susceptible people put out bowls of leftover pasta for them.

The damp air penetrated Flora's clothes. She tucked her scarf into the neck of her jacket and pulled the zip up.

It sure doesn't feel like spring yet.

At least it wasn't the bone-numbing cold of Chicago, where she'd gone to high school. "Spring" there meant waiting for her bus on a windy corner, ear muffs and scarf on and jumping up and down to stay warm. Several times, Flora had decided that Chicago was the coldest place on earth, especially when the wind roared down the tunnels formed by tall buildings looming over streets and sidewalks.

As she approached the river, she switched mental gears as she plotted how to insinuate her way into Vittorio's investigation.

It wouldn't be easy. Without an official role as a consultant to the Art Squad, Vittorio's colleagues wouldn't share information with her, or be interested in her opinions. At least Vittorio had agreed to keep their relationship secret as long as possible. That meant she could behave normally around the museum staff and to get to know them better as individuals. Flora hoped to pick up tidbits about staff backgrounds and employment histories.

She'd given her Uffizi job variation by alternating between long stints of bending over her work table and walking through the galleries to seek out potential conservation projects. The second task was not actually assigned to her, but Flora needed to stretch every hour or risk her lower back setting up like concrete in her chair. She found that her tours of the galleries cleared her mind and generated ideas. Staring at a misapplied varnish reminded her of tips for removing it. Identifying a pigment forced her to review the chemical composition of different colors over time.

Flora planned to use her gallery strolls to interact more with fellow staff members and uncover anything that might help the police.

First, she put in an hour at her work table so Giulia wouldn't breathe down her neck for goofing off. But Giulia approved of her wandering on her time off. Unlike the other staff, Flora didn't use her breaks for smoking and gossiping in the break room.

After gulping the last of the lukewarm coffee in her mug, she climbed the stairs and entered the Medieval section of the museum. Chiara Altavilla stood in the far corner, taking notes on a clipboard.

Aha! My chance to get to know her a bit...if she doesn't bite my head off first.

Flora crossed the gallery. "Chiara, *buon giorno.*"

The curator looked up, annoyed. "What are *you* doing up here?"

Hardly a welcoming tone of voice.

"I like to use my breaks to get to know the museum. And to make notes of possible conservation projects."

"I thought your job was to focus on the Renaissance paintings. After all, you won't be here very long." She tilted her nose up away from Flora and patted her elegant chignon.

Flora wondered if Chiara knew something she did not. Giulia and Ottavia, her boss back in Rome, had made a deal on loaning

Flora to the Uffizi for a month. She decided to ignore Chiara's hostile manner.

"A month is long enough to do quite a lot of work, and my boss will give me an extension if needed. Do you have any paintings that need attention in case I do have the time?"

Chiara's face softened a fraction. "Well, since you mention it, this Medieval wooden panel has some flaking paint...here, and here." She described the problems of the wall piece in front of them.

Flora took a few notes in her pocket-sized notebook. While her memory was sufficient for private notes, she preferred to put work-related notes on paper and then into a file that would detail her productivity while at the Uffizi. She'd found out the hard way that bosses liked accurate documentation—with dates to prove she met deadlines. She could be sloppy about housework at home, but not the conservation projects in her day job.

Chiara moved away, her heels tapping on the floor.

Flora followed her. "Chiara, how long have you worked here at the Uffizi?"

Chiara's dark eyebrows snapped together. "Three years. Why do you ask?"

"I'm always interested in other people's career paths. My own has been so circuitous, doing half my training in the United States and the other half over here."

The curator grunted. "Well, you can't say that about my path. Straight and uneventful. University of Bologna, graduate training in Rome, a job at the Villa Giulia, then here."

"The Villa Giulia!" exclaimed Flora. "Then you know my friend Assunta Vianello?"

"Assunta? Of course. She is a great colleague." Chiara's tone warmed. "I really enjoyed working with her."

"So did I. She helped us with...er, a Classical sculpture problem." Flora restrained herself from adding that the sculpture in question had turned out to be an excellent forgery.

"So, you treat sculptures as well as paintings?"

"Occasionally."

They chatted a few more minutes until Flora realized her break was over. "I have to get back to the lab. Perhaps you and I could have lunch someday soon?"

"I'm pretty busy this week. Maybe later in the month." Chiara walked briskly out of the gallery, leaving Flora feeling a bit foolish.

Inviting her to lunch was a mistake. This woman isn't really interested in forming new friendships now. Or ever.

But it didn't matter, Flora didn't have to make a friend out of Chiara. Just work with her a few more weeks.

She'd gleaned one useful bit of information: Chiara had been at the Uffizi for three years, long enough to know everyone who worked here.

But in Flora's humble opinion, Chiara made an unlikely suspect in the swap of the two Botticelli paintings.

Twelve

Flora decided to take a walk and then eat her sandwich at her worktable.

She headed north above the Piazza della Signoria toward a small wine bar in the Piazza Sant'Elisabetta she and Vittorio liked.

As she navigated the narrow sidewalks, dodging motorbikes and delivery trucks, Flora's mind wandered into new territory. Making forgeries was a source of income for someone, perhaps several people. What if there were more forgeries hanging on the walls of the Uffizi—forgeries created by the same hand as the Botticelli? How would a small team go about replacing original paintings with expert forgeries?

She tried to put herself into the mindset of a forger. What would she need to do such a job? First, free access to the original painting, with enough time to take careful measurements, study the style, the paint strokes, and the surface texture and to take detailed digital photos. What else? Well, to duplicate the colors convincingly, she'd need to mix up paints and make test strips of canvas or panel. Oh yeah—and research the correct pigments used by that artist working in a specific time period. A careful forger would usually plan ahead to fool art history so-called experts and scientists bent on pigment analysis.

Flora arrived at a tiny piazza charmingly situated with outdoor seating and two portable umbrellas that sat in front of the wine bar, *Antiche Dogane*. She took a break, perching on a cement barrier. Except for the pigeons cooing around her feet, she was in a rare oasis of quiet. The wine bar boasted a green vine crawling around the doorway. The door itself was a double wooden one, topped with a semi-circle of iron grillwork. Besides an excellent selection of Italian and French wines, the restaurant offered delicious plates of pasta, *panini*, and *antipasti* platters. It was a great place to go for a light meal when she didn't feel like cooking.

She resumed her musing. Assuming she was a forger with access to the painting she planned to copy, what about the timing of the work? Paintings owned by the Uffizi were either on display or in deep storage with lousy lighting. If the subject of the planned forgery were on display, she could take notes and discreet measurements in broad daylight, posing as an art student in full view of the museum guards. Flora already knew the guards didn't pay much attention to tourists unless they did something odd or threatening.

But if the target were in storage, she'd either need to "borrow" a stored painting for hours or days, risking someone discovering that the painting was missing from its appointed place, or choose a painting that was in transition. One that moved around the building at irregular intervals. That meant a new acquisition or a loan.

Either a new painting or a loan from another museum might visit Registration or the Conservation Lab—places where multiple staff members could have access to it—before it was carried to its exhibition gallery for installation.

Ah, but the installation of a new exhibit would provide the most opportunities. Especially in a massive museum like the Uffizi, where more than one temporary display was in progress at any given time. Multiple people were involved in such ventures: registrars, curators, plasterers, preparators, electricians…

A place like the new gallery being prepared for formerly stolen art work would be ideal.

Each piece in that exhibit was a loan from a different museum or private collector. The renovation of the gallery had already taken almost six months, long enough for all kinds of shenanigans.

Flora rose from her perch and turned back toward the river. It was fun to think herself into the mind of a forger, but not very useful unless more recent forgeries were discovered hanging on the walls of the Uffizi.

One key insight stuck in her mind. If a forger operated at the Uffizi, he needed to be either on the staff of the museum to gain access to artwork he wanted to copy, or have a buddy let him into the museum at odd hours.

It would be so much easier to complete his task if he spent every day in the Uffizi as a member of the staff—and kept his painting workshop in a hidden location very close by.

Thirteen

Flora returned to the Uffizi, entering the courtyard at the north end between the two wings and taking the ground floor back to the lab. This part of the building, facing the Arno river, was the oldest section of the former palace. Its rooms were originally designed as workshops and studios for court metalsmiths, jewelry artists, glassmakers, ceramicists, and tapestry makers. On the other side of the horseshoe, the west wing was the original mint where florins were coined. The *Fonderia*, or pharmacy, which manufactured perfumes, "miraculous" medicines, and poisons, was located nearby.

Hungry for her delayed lunch, Flora wondered what the duchess thought about the huge contrast between her workshop and archive phases and her time as an elegant gallery for the nobility...

The duchess was creaky today; her arthritis was bothering her. The walls made little whispering sounds as their foundations settled into the soft ground near the Arno. Window frames, especially the oldest ones, shifted in their holes as their wood rotted. Some hadn't been opened in years and would never open again.

She sighed and stretched a little, wishing all the nosy little people would leave her structure and stop bothering her. The tramping of tourists reminded her of the workshop days, when the hallways rocked with noise and smells of human trespassing. She was too old for this. So many signs of age in her bones, on her skin. The gilded plaster near her ceilings flaked, sending tiny bits onto the heads of unsuspecting staff and tourists. Damp seeped in between her joints, raising memories of the catastrophic flooding of 1966. Drafts eddied around stairwells, allowing cool air to waft in, mixing with the mustiness of ancient mildew…

Flora shook herself as she reentered the present. Ahead of her, she spied a tall young man with a satchel lurking near the entrance to her laboratory.

"May I help you?"

He turned to face her, a charming grin on his face. "No, I know my way around."

His tousled blond hair and delicately modeled features reminded her of someone. Who?

"Are you a frequent visitor?"

"I come sometimes to visit my cousin. He is one of the guards here."

She kept walking and he fell in step beside her.

"Do you work here?" he asked.

"Yes. I'm a visiting conservator, here for a few weeks."

He placed one hand on her arm, forcing her to stop and look at him. "I bet you are…a paintings specialist."

She laughed. "How could you know that? It's true, though."

"I knew it. You have the look of a connoisseur of paintings. A kind of listening look."

"Listening? I thought it was all about seeing." Flora found herself amused at this guy's unusual pickup patter. His hand still held her arm, gently, but there was nothing subtle about it. She detached herself.

He smiled. "Listening to the artist behind the painting. The intent, the technique, the choice of materials."

Intrigued, she gazed into his sky-blue eyes. "Actually, I do think about those things when I'm working on a painting. I feel I cannot be a good conservator unless I pay attention to the original painting under the varnish. The piece I was working on recently—" she stopped, aware she'd almost revealed something that was not public knowledge.

"What painting is this?"

She shook her head. "It's not important. Look, I must get back to work. The guard room is back that way." She pointed the way they had come.

"I know this." He turned and sauntered away, his jacket and satchel flung oh-so-casually over one shoulder.

"What's your name?" she called.

"Giorgio."

"I'm Flora."

Flora gave herself a mental shake. Really, she should not have been so chatty with a complete stranger. But he was so attractive... The feeling of having met Giorgio before remained.

Fourteen

No sooner did Flora enter the conservation lab than her phone rang.

"*Dottore* Romano wants us again. Meet you there."

The call was from Giulia.

Flora retraced her steps and turned right into the office area. The conference room door stood open and she could hear Romano's loud voice.

"...I intend to get to the bottom of this. Ah, here she is."

She took a seat next to Giulia, feeling a twinge of unease as she observed Romano's tight lips and the way he slapped his papers on the table. Only two other people were in the room: Chiara and Federico.

"You were all at the first meeting with the Carabinieri. Captain Bernini tried to convince me that his appearance at our door was because of a routine inspection, but I didn't believe him. Somebody called him. Who was it?"

His dark eyes glinted like obsidian as they focused on each face in turn.

No one spoke and the silence settled on the room like a thick layer of glue.

The director slammed his fist on the arm of his chair. "I demand to know who made that phone call!"

Giulia spoke first. "Flora gave me the contact information for Captain Bernini, but I didn't make the call. Flora told me about a week ago that she had a friend in the Art Squad."

"Miss Garibaldi, explain yourself."

"Giulia is correct. I know the captain from a murder case in Siena. You may have read about it."

"Not the Lorenzetti case?" Romano spat. "How did you get mixed up in that?"

"Signor Lorenzetti—the father—was my employer at a *restauro* in Siena. Bernini was a *tenente* at the time, working with a senior officer on the case."

Flora registered different expressions on her colleagues' faces: horror on Giulia's and smug satisfaction on Chiara's.

"You called him."

"Yes, but—"

Romano leaned across the table, his face purpling. "What gave you the right to call him in after you knew from our prior meeting that I wanted to gather all the information first?"

"I'm sorry, but Captain Bernini made it quite clear to me that art thefts require immediate attention. Statistically, police who secure a crime scene and begin their investigation on day one are most likely to have a successful outcome—particularly when portable antiquities or paintings are involved." Flora knew she sounded pompous, but Romano scared her.

Federico chimed in. "What she means is, our entire museum is a crime scene. The more we move around and touch things, the more we contaminate the evidence."

Flora glanced at him in surprise. His support gave her courage to continue. "Exactly. The Art Squad needs to be here from the beginning."

Especially if some of the people involved in the crime were members of the museum staff. Were they? Anyone could help by opening a door or hiding a painting temporarily.

"*Dottore*, there's something else we should consider," Giulia said. "The person or persons who exchanged the original Botticelli for the forgery could be part of the army of workmen—electricians, plasterers, painters—we've had here for months. I don't have any idea how many people have access to that gallery during the course of a week. Do you?"

Romano groaned. "No. I wish I did."

"What do we do now?" asked Federico.

The boss turned his hostile gaze toward Flora. "My first thought was to fire Miss Garibaldi, but she obviously knows Captain Bernini and he won't let that happen." He rubbed his head hard with one hand. "She stays. And everyone must cooperate with the police. Got it?"

Everyone nodded.

"Back to work, then." Romano scraped back his chair and exited the room without looking back.

Flora rose to her feet, which wobbled like cold linguini, and left the room. She descended the main staircase to the conservation lab.

The door to the lab was unlocked, not unusual at this time of day since people came and went and the lab was isolated from the construction area and the public entrance.

On the way to her work station, she stepped on something squishy. Looking down, she saw it was a tube of paint. Cadmium red, one of the most toxic and expensive of oil paints.

Her stomach clenching, she hurried to her work table. More squashed paint tubes, brushes flung on the floor, a trail of solvent on her table.

At least the Botticelli had been removed from the lab after questions about its authenticity arose. The Anthony van Dyck canvas she was currently restoring was untouched, as if the culprit had wanted to slow down Flora's work but possessed enough restraint not to harm the museum's collection.

A fellow museum staffer? Flora could think of a couple of prime candidates who disliked her: the two young Italians who worked under Giulia in Conservation, Alessandro Ferrari and Francesca Mancini. The woman was especially hostile, perhaps because she was so new to the job and had yet to be hired on a permanent basis. Flora had the impression she was dating Alessandro, who also resented Flora for no particular reason.

Why would either Francesca or Alessandro bother undermining the work of a temporary employee who would be gone in a few weeks? Sheer vindictiveness, or something more sinister?

Flora sat with a thud, staring at the mess and feeling the cold sweat break out on her back.

Maybe someone had figured out just how close her connection with the Carabinieri was and assumed she was spying for them. Or assumed she knew something about the exchange of the original Botticelli with the expert forgery. If that were the case, it must be someone more senior than the newest and youngest employee in conservation.

She gazed at the van Dyck, an oil portrait of the cardinal Guido Bentivoglio. His exquisitely rendered silk robes glowed red in the area where she'd already removed the yellowed varnish with solvent and cotton swabs.

Another thought occurred to her. Could the disruption of her work be a warning?

Stop investigating or I'll do something worse…

Fifteen

Bernini found interviewing the Uffizi guards uphill work.

Mario De Luca, the head guard, was a middle-aged guy with a burly build and ruddy skin, the telltale signs of good living and plenty of wine. The windowless closet he inhabited was in the oldest part of the ground floor of the palace, near the Palazzo Vecchio. Bernini glanced around, noticing a wall of cubbyholes stuffed with old magazines, coffee mugs, a crumpled sweater, and miscellaneous junk.

Without much hope, Bernini said, "*Signor* De Luca, what I really need is a calendar of guard assignments over the past month, up until the discovery of the fake Botticelli. Who was where, when. Do you have such a thing?" He thought that the switch of paintings could easily have taken place months earlier, but they had to start somewhere.

Mario scratched his curly head. "No, no. I use a clipboard, see? First, I grab two copies of a blank weekly schedule and stick one on my bulletin board—" He gestured at a section of wall crammed with notices, pictures, and newspaper ads. "I contact my guards and fill in the shifts according to availability. Then when I travel around the museum, I stick a second copy on my clipboard. When the week is over, I throw both copies away."

Really? Bernini thought, how strange—it looks like this guy never throws *anything* out. The scheduling sounded very haphazard and probably unfair to the employees; some could talk their way out of shifts because of family complications while others were stuck with extra hours. It also made the police job more complicated: no regular rotations of guards on a weekly or monthly basis.

"May I see your clipboard?"

Mario rummaged in the stacks on his desk and pulled it out.

Bernini perused it. Sure enough, some names appeared much more often than others. "How do you keep track of sick days and other absences?"

"Same system. I jot them down on the clipboard, then I throw it out after the monthly payday."

Bernini's eyebrows jumped as he wondered how the museum still functioned. Further questioning confirmed De Luca ran a loose ship, his operation dependent on camaraderie, nepotism, and good intentions. He knew who was where on any particular day but saw no need to keep track of past timetables. Bernini asked, "Do you have someone in charge of staff vacations and salary payouts?"

"Ask Diana Turchetti. She works in Administration. She keeps track of all that stuff. I call her once a month and give her the details of who missed a shift, then I throw out the papers."

Bernini flashed a glance at Esposito. Esposito got the message and left the room. He'd find this Diana and interview her, see if she kept a better paper trail.

"What about a record of when the alarm system was turned off, say for a part replacement or electrical upgrade?"

Mario stared. "Uh, that does happen, but I don't remember exactly. When it does, I get a phone call. I turn the system off when they tell me to, then I turn it back on. No need to write that down, is there? The new computerized system is supposed to record that data anyway."

Another job for Esposito, thought Bernini. He could obtain printouts from the server and check them.

"Tell me how the alarm system works," he said.

Mario brightened. "Aw, now we're talking! We have such a good system. There are doorway alarms for entering or leaving the building, alarms for opening a case without authorization, alarms for entering certain storage areas—"

"Whoa! Start with what *kind* of system you have: is it all cameras and CCTV? Do you have infrared? Do you have motion detectors?"

"All of those things, in different parts of the building..." Mario described them in excruciating detail as he gave Vittorio a tour.

It took almost three hours.

~ * ~

At the end of it, Bernini had a pounding headache and an unusual feeling of helplessness.

As he crossed the piazza with Esposito for a drink, preferably a double espresso, his mind spit out a depressing list of obstacles.

Bernini would not have extolled the alarm system as "good." It was a piece of crap, archaic, useless. Multiple alarms existed, yes, but not on every door. So many little rooms and alcoves were accessible, perfect for hiding things—or people. In the oldest part of the palace, some doors had no locks. Those that did have locks had no keys—they had gone missing decades or centuries ago. The Uffizi had been a multipurpose building for over four hundred years.

The security cameras were gradually being replaced, but many were years old with software that didn't mesh with the newer installations. Sections of the museum not open to the public—used by museum staff for office and laboratory space—had no cameras at all. Bernini knew the new Conservation Lab would have cameras, but that was months in the future.

The closed-circuit TV system was also being replaced, on an

unknown timetable. That meant large parts of it had been off for the past several months.

Esposito fetched their coffees while Bernini rearranged a table and chairs so they sat in the back of the cafe, facing staff and other clients. They couldn't be overheard.

"What did you find out from Diana?" Bernini asked.

Esposito's brown eyes danced. "She's worth her considerable weight in gold. She told me that Pietro, Mario's assistant, is the one who actually tracks staff movements—as much as anyone can in this place. Mario hands over his scraps of paper when he remembers to, but Pietro keeps his own schedule and he's the one who sends in the monthly reports." He put a sheaf of paper on the table.

Bernini's mood lightened as he flicked through the pages. "Maybe we can make some progress after all, despite the fact that Mario De Luca deploys his staff unevenly, with no recognizable pattern."

"That sucks. One other thing you should know. There are two periods each day when the main alarm system is turned off: at the beginning of the day when staff arrive but the public is not allowed in, and at the end of the day, same thing."

"Hmm." Most museums worked that way. Someone posing as a staff member or construction member wanting to sneak in—or out— had two obvious windows of opportunity. But the staff had IDs. Did the construction workers? Bernini made a note on his pad.

Esposito added, "And the guard who's supposed to watch the camera in the morning often runs out to get coffee during those times. On the other hand, the Uffizi has several guards posted at night, so they have almost twenty-four/seven coverage."

Bernini nodded. "Night coverage is becoming more common for big museums, especially in this country."

Esposito continued. "You won't like this: no one can find computerized records for when the alarms were turned off in the

Botticelli wing over the past two years. If it existed, it's been wiped from the system. Also, I spoke to the head electrician Carlo, and he's like Mario…he does what he's told, but he finds no reason to write down a daily schedule. The construction chief employs several contractors beside the electrician. For example, the air conditioning team comes in from Siena and has clearance to go all over the museum as needed."

Bernini grimaced. "This is the case from hell! Our time frame for the crime is up to two years ago then?"

"Yeah, but it's complicated. Remember, there's a new computer system that's only one year old, and that one doesn't mesh with the previous one."

Bernini rolled his eyes. "The gallery renovation includes modernizing the security systems, but that's been ongoing for ten years and counting. I defy anyone to keep track of all the changes. Personnel aside, the main problem is this ancient building. It's like a labyrinth, especially in older sections of the palace on the other side of the building from the new staircases, gift shop, and restrooms."

"Maybe the security system is not the major issue. Isn't it true that most of the recent thefts dealt with by the Carabinieri have been low-tech—that is, events that don't involve turning off the alarms? I remember at least one case where a thief entered in the late afternoon during public visiting hours and stayed behind. He found a place to hide overnight and then exited in the morning carrying a small painting under his coat."

"Yes…that theft happened in Berlin. Another scenario is a thief enters the museum legally, hides, grabs a piece of art, and then breaks a window to exit. Guards rush around trying to find out who entered the museum while the guy escapes." He gazed approvingly at his assistant. "Problem is, this theft is different. We don't even know when the Botticelli original was replaced with the forgery, so how the hell can we pinpoint where people were at the crucial time?"

Esposito nodded. "There's one ray of hope. Most of the security staff has been here at least five years. Only two men were hired in the past two years. I can begin with making a chart of their shifts and vacation days as far back as this record goes, but I'll need some help."

"Call the main office and get the people you need up here. I'll put some of them on staff interviews and assign one to help you with your chart. Then, I can focus on the other million-Euro question."

"Sir?"

"Where is the original Botticelli now?"

Sixteen

The Carabinieri were sniffing around the operations of the museum, scrutinizing guard movements and timetables. The Boss would not be happy.

How could he, a lowly employee, counteract such police efficiency? By appearing to cooperate while withholding vital information. Such as how many people moved around the museum at night—when the alarm system was armed.

The Boss had set it up so three guards traded one day shift for an all-nighter, one per week. These lucky minions did the Boss's bidding in certain sections of the building, while the sucker on duty moved around on a set path at predetermined intervals. Like clockwork, the chess pieces moved around the Uffizi, one half not knowing what the other half was doing.

The system worked because the Boss made it clear that any deviation would have dire consequences. Not only would the culprit lose his or her job, but he might just disappear.

You'd think a painting as large as the Birth of Venus would be hard to hide. Still in its frame, it would be. But stripped from the frame and rolled up, it was just a tube—one that fit inside PVC pipes, or packing materials that were strewn around the construction areas.

You could move a stolen work of art in broad daylight by posing as a construction worker. No one knew that better than him, the man in charge of the Botticelli swap.

Seventeen

Flora mulled over her day as she sautéed onions and mushrooms for her own version of the French chicken stew, *coq au vin*, that Vittorio liked so much. The additions of several kinds of mushrooms and red wine—lots of it—increased the savory mouth-feel of the dish. It tasted even better accompanied with crusty Italian bread and a hearty red wine for sipping.

Romano's reaction, nasty as it was, to Flora's interference with the Carabinieri made sense; the director was obviously a man who believed he should always be in control. He hated feeling helpless...or upstaged.

The sabotage of Flora's work station worried her more, since it might be connected to the investigation and her role in it.

Would Vittorio insist she quit asking questions and distance herself from the police investigation during the remainder of her time at the museum? That would be difficult for Flora, but better than being suddenly transferred back to Rome. She was involved, for better or worse. At least Vittorio could protect her from Romano's wrath by making sure she wasn't fired because she was helping the Carabinieri.

The raw onions made her eyes water, so she dumped them into the sauce and moved over to her second cutting board to prepare the garlic. The savory smells of cooking filled the apartment, and out of nowhere, Gattino appeared and rubbed himself against her legs.

"Darn cat!" Flora muttered as the little animal almost tripped her. But actually, she was delighted that Vittorio had brought the pint-sized black cat up from Rome for her. That meant he had wrestled Gattino into his carrier all by himself. Since the cat was an accomplished escape artist, that was no mean feat.

How could she reassure Vittorio and keep herself as part of the investigation? She'd tell him about Chiara's on-again, off-again coolness toward her and the lack of enthusiasm in other staff members for her presence. It was certainly possible that one of them wanted her gone before her conservation tasks were complete.

Vittorio would focus on how Flora might be in danger if the thief or forger thought Flora was getting too close to a discovery about the missing Botticelli. Flora thought the crime complicated enough that it must involve at least two people...maybe more.

She tipped the chopped garlic into the saucepan, along with a handful of fresh basil and thyme and a cup and a half of red wine. Then she added a second half-cup, figuring the stew had at least an hour to simmer and most of the wine would boil away.

As her hands moved automatically to fill a pot with water, her mind tilted in a new direction: Flora felt herself being pulled away from her conservation work into the police investigation and the complicated relationships of the people around her at the Uffizi. What did this mean? Was painting restoration beginning to take second place to the rest of her life?

The sound of a key turning in the lock alerted Gattino that his master was home. He raced for the front door for the usual ceremonies of head-butting and leg-rubbing.

She heard Vittorio greeting the cat and dumping his briefcase and keys on the bench near the door.

"Hi," he said, striding into the kitchen and kissing the back of her neck. "Oh, that smells good."

"Hi, yourself," she said, turning to kiss him properly. "Pour us some wine?"

"What would you like tonight?" He entered the small pantry where Flora kept a rack for wine bottles. "A merlot or a chianti?"

"I opened a merlot already for the stew," she said, pointing with her potato peeler. "We can drink that. There's a second bottle if we need it. I have to add the veggies, then I'll sit down."

He sat with his wine glass. "How was your day?"

"Er...terrible." She told him about Romano and the attack on her workstation.

Vittorio reacted as she expected. "I've taken care of the director—he can't fire you—but the attack on your conservation materials has got to be connected to our investigation. You had no such episodes during your first few weeks here."

"True, but I was an unknown element when I first arrived—no one had any reason to dislike me or want to cause me difficulties." She added the chopped potatoes to boiling water and set a timer. Once the potatoes were cooked, she'd mash them with garlic and butter to complement the stew. She sank into the seat opposite Vittorio.

"But the discovery of the theft and replacement of the Botticelli, followed by the arrival of the Carabinieri, closely preceded the attack on you."

"Not an attack on my person," she reminded him. "Just my workstation. I was never in danger." Flora eyed him carefully.

Vittorio's smile vanished and his eyebrows hunched together. "These things can escalate, you know. First an attack on your stuff, then an attack on you, perhaps as a warning to me."

She leaned forward as if she could persuade him by being physically closer. "Only if it's widely known that we're a couple, so the culprit thinks harming me might deter the police. And so far, Giulia is the only one who suspects our true relationship."

"Hmm."

"The fact that the painting I was working on was not damaged implies it was another member of the staff. Someone who wanted to slow me down, maybe frighten me into keeping my mouth shut."

Vittorio nodded, his hazel eyes watchful. "I agree. No staff member in his or her right mind would risk damaging a painting…it would mean instant dismissal."

"Usually, yes. But I'm only a temporary employee, so whoever did it probably thinks the risk of dismissal is less for him or her."

"Or you're more widely disliked than you think." Then he smiled. "Which I think is unlikely."

Flora told him about her interactions with Chiara and Alessandro. "Both of them dislike me." She rose to stir the stew and turn down the heat under the potatoes.

Vittorio's cell phone rang. "Esposito, how's it going?" He wandered into their small living room to talk privately while she set the table and filled water glasses. Aware that she liked her wine a bit too much, Flora had decided to drink more water with every meal.

"Guess what," he said, returning to the table. "We have our first real lead in the Botticelli theft."

"Can you tell me?"

"I'd better not. But it means we are looking outside the museum for our culprit."

His phone rang again. This time she saw his expression change and his mouth tighten. He paced the hallway, and all she could hear was his voice without understanding his replies.

When he returned, slipping his cell phone back into his pocket, she asked, "Now what?"

"I've got to go back to Rome," said Vittorio. "There's a major fight brewing in how to manage another international incident: vandalism by a crazy Frenchman of Michelangelo's *Pietà* at St. Peter's."

She stared. "How on earth did anyone do that? Was it in broad daylight?"

"You'd be surprised what people will do to get publicity."

"How unfortunate. Just when you've barely got started here."

He rubbed his eyes. "You're so right. I have to leave Esposito in charge of the interviews, and I'm sure the *Polizia di Stato* here in Florence will have some say in how things are conducted." He looked at Flora. "You'd best lie low while I'm gone. The others won't take kindly to what they see as interference from a civilian— even such a pretty one as you."

Flora grimaced. "Don't bother to flatter me. I know only too well how your colleagues view me: a necessary nuisance. And they won't feel obligated to treat me, the boss's girlfriend, nicely with you out of the way." Privately, she felt a jolt of unease. Would Esposito restrict her movement around the museum? Would the *Polizia di Stato* interview her?

He glanced at his phone to check the time. "Could we eat early? I have to catch the train at twenty-two hundred."

"Sure, I just have to mash the potatoes. You know, Esposito doesn't like me much. I'll have to work to change his mind."

"I think he's a little jealous of our relationship."

"Great. Now I have two strikes against me: I'm your girlfriend and I'm an interfering snoop."

And privately she added to herself, *I bet Esposito and the others would treat me better if I were a policeman too.*

Eighteen

Flora arrived at work the next day with some trepidation. She really didn't want to run into Esposito, or anyone else from the police now that the museum staff knew of her previous connection with the Carabinieri. "Police stooge" was the kindest epithet she was likely to receive, and the uppity duo of Chiara and Alessandro would surely come up with worse things to call her.

Since she was early, she chose a gallery of early Sienese art for her first stroll of the day. Flora moved slowly around the room, marveling as she had before at the slightly green flesh of the painted Virgin Marys. Flora remembered that tint was due to underpainting with a green earth, *terre verte*, made from the minerals glauconite and celadonite. It certainly made her think of corpses rather than live people, but fourteenth century painters in Italy often used the pigment for human flesh.

The early fourteenth century wooden-framed work, *Madonna and Child* by Duccio drew her attention, with its enigmatic, slightly sinister Madonna with her adult-looking Child. The woman's inward-looking gaze was emphasized by the slanted, almost oriental eyes. The baby reached up one arm toward her ear, a charming gesture, more realistic than anything else in the painting.

Flora moved closer to examine the tempera. Unlike the now infamous Botticelli, this painting showed the original luminous colors overlaid with the dulling films of time. She wondered when the picture had last been cleaned and made a note to check.

Footsteps behind her made her turn. Esposito confronted her, leaning in close enough to make her personal space feel small.

"Snooping again?" he sneered.

"No. I'm getting more familiar with the galleries so I can do my job better—"

"Why would you need to do that? You're a temporary employee, soon to be sent back to Rome where you belong."

Flora hated being interrupted, especially when engaged in her private pursuits. It reminded her of an American piano teacher who had grabbed her wrist during lessons. He never let her play the pieces she had practiced all the way through before he began dissecting her technique.

She smiled like the Cheshire cat in *Alice in Wonderland*. "Actually, this gallery is extremely relevant to my conservation work. The paintings belong to the same period as the Botticelli that was stolen, the one I was working on before I discovered it is a forgery."

Esposito responded by showing his own teeth. "Ah, yes. Your limited experience with tempera makes you a world-class expert."

She realized he was baiting her, trying to make her say something regrettable. Wishing she could actually disappear at will like the famous cat, she said, "I studied under a *world-class* expert from St. Petersburg. He taught us how to mix our own tempera paints and showed us how each color looked as it aged in different light and temperature conditions. Great training for what I'm doing here in this museum."

Esposito's face revealed a flicker of respect, but his tone of voice was still sharp. "Shouldn't you be in the laboratory? What will your boss say?"

She could score a point. "Giulia approves of my gallery walks. She wishes all her employees would show such interest in the collections. And I'm still early since we don't start work until eight-thirty."

She marched away from him, intent on visiting the staff coffee machine and retreating out of the range of the testy officer.

"Wait, Flora. I—"

"*Signorina* Garibaldi to you, *Tenente*. Only my friends call me Flora." She kept walking.

A tall man in the blue and gray uniform of the *Polizia di Stato* passed her and buttonholed Esposito.

"*Tenente* Esposito? We need to talk." She stopped within earshot, curious because of the man's harsh tone.

"*Si, signore.*"

"It's *Ispettore* Grandesso to you. Where's Bernini? He was supposed to meet me half an hour ago."

"He had to return to Rome."

"And I suppose he left you in charge? Well, let me tell you how things actually work around here. I'm in charge of any investigation involving the Uffizi—"

Flora permitted herself an evil little chuckle. Esposito the Jerk deserved a taste of his own medicine. He'd see how much *he* liked being belittled for just doing his job!

She wondered how this interference would affect Vittorio's plans. The local police didn't always get along with the Carabinieri. She'd better tell Vittorio about this incident in their next phone call.

Wait a minute. Disagreement between two branches of the Italian police could work in her favor: Vittorio would need her eyes and ears even more than before.

Especially if the Florence division of the *Polizia di Stato* had no idea she had an in with the Carabinieri.

Nineteen

A timid sun rose over the waterlogged city of kings and emperors. The Roman streets looked washed after the pounding rains of yesterday. As cafes and fruit sellers rattled up their metal grates, the local cats crept out of their hidden lairs to hunt for food.

Vittorio Bernini, feeling surly and rumpled after an overnight ride on a noisy train, took a taxi to the apartment he shared with Flora in Trastevere—the older section of the city across the Tiber River—to shower and shave. As he climbed out of the taxi, he smelled the peculiar odor of Rome: stagnant water, cat piss, and overcooked garlic.

Slightly refreshed after soaking in hot water, he wrapped a towel around his waist and padded into the tiny kitchen to brew an espresso. While he waited for the water to boil, he called the *Caserma* for a ride to the office. He'd prefer walking, but he was running late and his boss would be waiting.

He wondered how Esposito was doing with the new information he'd reported the previous evening. A known antiquities smuggler appeared on the list of official visitors a month before Flora's identification of the forgery. That meant if the original painting had been removed from the museum at that time, then the trail was cold. But it gave the Carabinieri a direction to search: their focus must be on how a smuggler could gain access to the Uffizi despite the large guard presence day and night.

Bernini very much hoped Esposito wasn't making Flora miserable. The interactions he'd observed between them suggested that Esposito was both jealous and hostile. Jealous of Vittorio's relationship with Flora, and hostile toward Flora because of her obvious intelligence and superior knowledge about art history and conservation.

Esposito came from a traditional Tuscan farming community, Vescovado di Murlo, near Siena. Women cooked, cleaned, and bore babies while the men did the important work, the planting and harvesting of crops and wine-making. His coarse jokes and awkward flirtations showed how uncomfortable he was with professional women, especially those at his level and above, in the police.

A ping on his phone told Bernini his ride was waiting. He grabbed his suit jacket and keys, slid the cell into his pocket, and locked the apartment.

The young officer waiting in the Alfa Romeo (black with red stripes) said very little, leaving Bernini alone with his thoughts. They ranged from noting parking violations—*another* mini-car parked at right angles to the other parked cars, just asking to be crushed by a passing motorcycle—to wondering just how long the urgent case would keep him away from Florence and Flora.

The car sped through the neighborhood, passing his favorite fresh pasta shop on the left and a woman placing a bowl of leftovers behind a parked car for the stray cats. In this part of Trastevere, the occasional sidewalks were narrow and bumpy, barely wide enough for one person to pass cars and dumpsters.

At the office, Bernini hurried up the wide stairs of the former palace to the conference room where his boss and colleagues were sipping coffee and swapping greetings.

"Bernini! How was the train? You could have driven faster back and forth," joked Captain Martini. Martini was the colleague Bernini knew best. They'd worked on several cases together.

"Not compared to the fast train. I shaved off fifteen minutes and didn't have any traffic.

"Bet you're glad to be home. Oh, but you had to leave the lovely Flora behind, so maybe not."

"She had a job to finish," Bernini growled. "So how much damage did the mad Frenchman do to the statue?"

His boss answered. "He took a mallet to the head of the Pietà. It will need extensive restoration."

"How did he get close enough to do it in the first place?"

"Knocked down a guard and jumped over the rope and stanchions."

The general called the meeting to order and the officers settled down to listen and trade reports. After half an hour, they dispersed with new assignments.

Bernini checked in at his office to read emails and answer phone calls before heading over to St. Peter's Basilica to review security procedures.

One email caught his attention. A colleague had written a message telling Bernini that the *Polizia di Stato* in Florence were conducting an investigation into construction fraud that included the Uffizi. Lorenzo Grandesso was in charge. "Thought you might need this info since Grandesso has been a thorn in your side in the past."

A huge, prickly thorn, thought Bernini. Grandesso had inserted himself into multiple investigations in and around Siena while Bernini had served as a junior officer prior to his transfer to Rome. Grandesso belonged to the type of officer who knew nothing, but assumed everything, causing havoc for fellow officers and underlings who preferred to follow established procedure.

He called Esposito's cell, but Esposito did not pick up. Bernini left a terse message, asking if Grandesso had made an appearance yet.

Then he called for his driver and sped over to Vatican City.

Twenty

Since Romano's dramatic questioning of her motives and actions, Flora had kept her head down and performed her work as well as she could. When engaged in less demanding tasks such as cleaning her brushes or mixing pigments, she racked her brain for ways to snoop without attracting too much attention from her colleagues.

Despite her efforts to be discreet, certain conversations stopped when she came near. Flora felt both isolated and frustrated, especially with Vittorio away in Rome.

While setting up her workstation for the next restoration project two days after her encounter with Esposito, she suddenly had an idea. What if the original Botticelli had never left the museum? It could be hidden in storage areas, behind other paintings or tucked among canvases of a similar size—not that there were too many paintings that large. She resolved to use her breaks to visit spaces closed to the public.

She'd been told the Uffizi was about halfway through the current renovation. Besides the new staircases, the workmen were finishing a new elevator block and enlarging the area that served as both bookstore and gift shop on the ground floor.

The former palace was a labyrinth, made even more complex by closures of key rooms and passageways for construction. Flora knew the basic layout of the former State Archives and Conservation on the ground floor, offices and labs on both ground floor and first floor, and most of the art galleries on the second floor. She also knew that many rooms were closed off, or stuffed with old state government archives—another target for a comprehensive search. Flora could gain access to the construction areas, perhaps by taking a tour with a bored guard, or better still, getting to know the head of construction, Graziano Ronzano.

During her first week, as Giulia had given her a tour, Flora had asked for a map.

"Map? We don't have any besides what the tourists get when they buy their tickets. Besides, anything obtainable now is already out-of-date since the construction guys move walls and doorways—not to mention staircases—on an almost weekly basis. You just have to memorize the basic layout and your daily route between lab, meeting room, and coffee machine." Giulia had smiled, obviously putting special weight on the location of her favorite beverage.

There must be maps of the building from different periods, Flora thought. If she could find them, she could narrow down areas to search and contribute something really helpful to the police investigation.

Flora had chatted once or twice with Ronzano. Perhaps if she visited him now, he would have current plans to show her?

She grabbed her coffee cup and keys and headed up the Grand Staircase to the main construction zone.

A cloud of plaster dust met her as she ventured into the room where drywall was being cut with the shriek of saws.

Ronzano, huddled with two workers, raised his head and smiled, holding up a hand to indicate he'd be free in a few minutes.

Flora mentally rehearsed what she'd say. When he approached, she was ready. "*Signore* Ronzano, during my breaks I explore the Uffizi so I can understand it better. I realized I have no idea which parts of the building are the oldest and how it is being changed. I don't want to take up much of your time, but—"

"But of course, *signorina*, I can show you here." He led her over to a table covered with blueprints and notepads. "See, the basic plan is to build a new staircase to send the tourists down to the first floor after they have visited the galleries on the second floor. We are encasing that staircase now. Then we finish the new restrooms that are half-constructed and create new offices just here." He pointed to a spot on the east wing of the U-shaped palazzo. "The second suite of offices is in the west wing, as you know."

"What about the new conservation laboratory?" She leaned over the table.

"It will be here." He explained how windows would be placed facing the Piazza del Grano and spent another ten minutes describing other renovations to improve both the public visitor experience and the working conditions of the museum staff. He cemented Flora's understanding of just how comprehensive the modern renovations were, and how complicated. No wonder each phase took eight to ten years.

Flora was ecstatic over the wealth of information he volunteered so freely. She itched to filch her own copy of the plans so she could compare it to older plans of the museum. But someone might ask awkward questions if she gave into that impulse. Maybe some of the renovation plans were in the museum staff library or online? She asked Ronzano.

"Certainly," he answered. "The Ministry of Cultural Assets and Activities published some of them. You can look them up at this address." He scribbled something on a piece of paper and handed it to her. "So, you find the renovations interesting?"

"I do. Especially since you told me our decrepit conservation lab will move up to the first floor where there is more space and much better natural light! Thank you so much."

He laughed and turned back to his colleagues.

Flora decided to make a quick stop at the so-called staff library on her way back to the laboratory.

There was no librarian, or catalog of the modest collection of gallery guides and exhibit plans piled on the few shelves. From the lack of order, Flora deduced that no one was assigned to keep track of the collection, at least until the renovations were complete. Ronzano had mentioned a later addition of a research center, but nothing about books and journals that might be housed there. Probably most departments had their own stash of useful publications, just like the conservation lab did.

Closing the small room, which was unlocked, Flora returned to the lab and fired up her laptop. The other conservators, Alessandro and Francesca, were out of the room on break, so she could spend a few minutes searching for plans online.

Bingo. A Google image search pulled up several older plans of the Uffizi. Flora copied a few to a Word document that she could print, to examine later, back at her apartment.

Half an hour later, well after Flora had abused her printer privileges, Alessandro hurried into the lab.

"Flora! A guard has just been found dead in the new gallery."

"Oh, how awful! You mean in Temporary Exhibits?"

"Yes." Alessandro's normally ruddy complexion had turned pale green, almost like a Sienese Madonna. He gulped. "It looks like foul play, and no one knows if he died this morning or last night."

"Is the guard someone you know?"

"Yes, he's a friend of mine, that's what makes it so unbearable. It's Davide Grandesso, nephew of the State Police inspector who's been making such a nuisance of himself. You should come with me right now. The police want to interview all the staff, and there's a painting that Chiara wants you to examine right away."

Twenty-one

Flora followed Alessandro out of the lab to the nearby new gallery—a space carved out of former storage rooms. The exhibit included paintings, sculpture, jewelry, and other works recovered from various art thefts all over Europe.

She had a moment to reflect that Alessandro was far too upset to show his usual antagonism toward her. Then they joined other museum staff clustered in an uneasy group at the back wall. Open display cases stood next to empty plinths. Half the paintings were hung; the others leaned against walls along with lonely sculptures, all waiting for the curator to position them. Stacks of labels sat on a long table, and stepladders and sculpture pedestals impeded movement. The strong smells of fresh paint and something metallic—blood?—filled Flora's nostrils.

A harassed-looking Esposito and another officer stood near the side wall, conferring and taking notes. The uncovered body lay next to the tipped-over guard's chair near the entrance. A police photographer recorded the grisly sight of the dead man lying in his own blood.

Flora felt her stomach lurch and looked away. Bile rose in her esophagus and threatened to choke her.

"Someone slit his throat," whispered one of the guards.

Someone was dead. Violently.

The Uffizi would never be the same. This crime would follow the staff into history.

Vittorio will say it's too dangerous now for me to be involved.

But I am already involved.

She shivered and looked around at the other staff.

Chiara, who had discovered the body, was white-faced and tight-lipped. She leaned against a wall, clutching a small painting. She fastened her gaze on Flora and motioned her over.

"Flora, I've found another peculiar painting," Chiara whispered.

As much as Flora wanted to think about something—anything—in the world besides the murder, she knew this was not the time. She spied Esposito approaching the nervous group of staff.

"Later," Flora whispered to Chiara.

Esposito loomed at her elbow. His harsh voice brought her rudely back into the present. "*Signorina,* when did you last see Grandesso?"

"Uncle or nephew?"

"Nephew. The dead nephew."

She cast her mind back. "Yesterday. I think."

"Can't you be more precise?"

Flora glared at him. "I cover a lot of ground every day and see many staff members on a regular basis. It's hard to remember unless we had a conversation, which we did not. I can't remember ever talking with him."

"Try a little harder. You'll be called for a proper interview."

Fine, she thought. Flora had nothing to contribute to the investigation, so Esposito's grilling wouldn't bother her. And she'd certainly tell Vittorio his colleague had been unnecessarily harsh with her. In the meantime, she had questions of her own, beginning with how the murder related to the stolen Botticelli. Had the guard known something that led to his death?

Feeling shaky and disoriented, she longed for the relative

privacy of the lab where the other staff couldn't judge every gesture she made, every expression flitting across her face.

She returned to the other side of the gallery while Esposito questioned Giulia, waiting for Esposito to dismiss them.

~ * ~

Later that afternoon, Flora went in search of Chiara in the office area on the first floor.

Chiara perched on a stool near her bulletin board, unpinning notices and notes she'd posted to keep herself on track.

"Oh, it's you." Chiara seemed to have recovered somewhat from her shock. She hopped off her stool and picked up the artwork from her desk. "Take a look and see what you think." Her expression of anticipation said she was testing Flora's art historical knowledge as well as her ability as a conservator.

Flora took the painting from Chiara's hands and turned it toward the overhead light so she could see it properly.

The backing was copper...how unusual. The portrait was very familiar. Surely this was a Rembrandt, a self-portrait? Then she recognized it.

"Isn't this the Rembrandt self-portrait stolen from Norway?"

"The National Museum of Stockholm. Very good, Flora," said Chiara drily. "But is it really a Rembrandt?"

Flora handled the framed portrait gingerly, holding it up to her eyes and then moving it closer to the natural light coming through the window. She leaned closer. Something was not quite right about the paint strokes in the upper right quadrant. And some of the color choices were unusual...was that yellow a normal pigment for a Rembrandt?

"I need to compare it to the other Rembrandts in the Dutch gallery. Is it okay if I take it out of the frame?"

"Please do whatever you must, but do it soon. I am not happy about this painting—I'm not sure it belongs in the new exhibit of stolen and recovered objects."

"I can see why. Several things bother me."

"It could be a forgery?"

"Yes, maybe. I want to look at the surface and the edges with my magnifying glasses. I'll take it back to the lab and return it to you in the next day or so. Okay?"

"Fine. Be sure and write me a short report in case I have to break bad news to Romano."

"Will do."

Flora hoped it was not another forgery, but instead the work of a student of Rembrandt rather than the master. That would require some reshuffling of the collection and how it was displayed, but not the kind of scandal they already had with the Botticelli.

The sinking feeling in her gut told her it would be tricky either way. Chiara might have to break the bad news, but Flora would be the one called on the carpet to justify her findings.

Twenty-two

Her cell phone rang just after she'd returned to the lab and placed the painting on her worktable. It was Vittorio.

"Esposito called me about the murder of Grandesso's nephew. Are you okay?"

Flora sighed. "I'm fine. Shaky, but fine. I'm still not used to dead bodies, especially when there's a lot of blood."

"No one really gets used to it. Those of us who see it often learn to put a mask of indifference on, but I still get nauseous."

"I suppose that's reassuring in a way—you don't take violent death for granted," she said. "By the way, Esposito acts like I am a thorn in his side every chance he gets. He's been behaving like a super jerk."

Vittorio sighed. "I'll tell him to lay off."

"I hate being here without you. When will you be back?"

"A murder changes everything. The powers that be have decided I can return tonight. They even okayed a car and a driver for me. So, expect me about twenty-three hundred."

Her sigh of relief was audible to both of them. "See you then. I hope you have a good driver."

"He's good, but *you* would say he drives too fast."

Flora disconnected and put the cell in her pocket. She was glad she hadn't told Vittorio about the second possible forgery. No point

84

in involving him until she'd completed her examination and had something concrete to tell him.

Now for the painting. Was it a Rembrandt, a work by one of his students, or a modern forgery? Not that easy to tell, even for connoisseurs of Dutch painting.

She remembered how the experts from the Netherlands Rembrandt Research Project were hated and feared by the museums they visited. Those highly trained scholars and scientists examined paintings with special instruments, poring over every detail. Disgraced former Rembrandts, now labeled "Student of Rembrandt," were removed from honored positions in popular galleries and hidden in basements.

Flora looked away from the portrait, thinking. One of her undergraduate teachers had sparked a passionate discussion on forgeries vs. copies. If the artist himself admired copies, what did that do to the concept of authenticity? Rembrandt himself encouraged his students to copy him. He modified the student paintings, selling some as official Rembrandts and others as authorized copies. One of Flora's teachers, an art historian, had quoted Picasso saying something like, if a forgery of his work was a good one, he'd be thrilled. He'd sit right down and sign it. She wished she could remember the exact words. To what degree were all such paintings "authentic?"

It was a totally different issue from good paintings that were created as deliberate forgeries. Flora could accept that a student of Rembrandt might paint something in the master's workshop that was partly authentic, because student methods and materials were heavily influenced by the master painter himself. But a professional forger— someone who copied other artists for deliberate gain—that was despicable. And criminal.

Federico Armani wandered into the lab. Flora liked him, and he seemed to find her opinions valuable.

"Federico, I'm thinking about how museums and collectors devalue paintings that were not created by the master, but by his students."

He perched his skinny butt on the end of her big table.

"Of course. It's all about the money. A painting by a student never fetches as much dough as one by the master."

"Yes, but I'm thinking more about the philosophical aspects of how you judge artworks. Is a really good painting less valuable to the history of art because a student of Rembrandt did it instead of Rembrandt himself?"

He smiled. "Ah, now you're in deep waters. I assume you're referring to the recent article about the reclassification of Rembrandts?"

"It does seem ironic that some artworks previously labeled 'Student of Rembrandt,' now attributed to Rembrandt himself, are suddenly back in the limelight. Not to mention these works are deemed more valuable, just because the labeling has changed overnight."

"You mean, the paintings come back out of storage and onto the gallery walls. So, may I watch while you examine this one?" He nodded at the small portrait in front of her.

"Be my guest."

Carefully, she loosened the screws that held the frame—a nineteenth-century gold gilt wooden frame—from the copper backing..

Donning her magnifying visor, she examined the surface. Rembrandt's palette included several common pigments—lead white, bone black, charcoal black, ochres, azurite, yellow lake, and vermillion. What she could see didn't match those on the Rembrandts she had reviewed on the way back from the murder scene.

She stood and invited Armani to take her place. "Take a look."

He sat and peered through the visor. "I don't like any of the colors, but the green is weird."

"I agree. These don't look like Rembrandt's usual choices. And some of the varnish looks recent as well—no yellowing."

They changed places.

She focused on the edges of the canvas. No telltale swatches of paint on two sides. But the third and fourth sides revealed trial patches of paint that matched the colors in the quadrant she found suspicious.

"Uh-oh."

"What?"

Then she saw the tiny happy face; it was the same graffito she'd found on the Botticelli.

"It's another forgery. By the same artist who painted the fake Botticelli."

He eyed her soberly. "I remember, Miss Flora, that you said once you thought forgeries should be on view along with authentic pieces, to provide education for visitors and students of art history."

Flora smoothed her curly hair with shaking hands. "That might be appropriate in a university art gallery, but I'm not sure the Uffizi would ever agree to do that. And I think forgeries should never be displayed for a long time—it gives them too much prominence."

"Correct. Tourists come to Firenze from far away to see original paintings. They'd feel cheated if they discovered they were looking at forgeries. And our dear director will not be happy about this new fiasco."

"He'll go ballistic."

"I will accompany you to tell him. That way his wrath will fall on both of us, not just you."

"That's kind of you, Federico. Thanks."

~ * ~

Armani left the lab to run an errand. He said they could visit Romano together as soon as he returned, in about an hour.

Flora scrabbled in her tote bag for her coffee flask. She checked the contents: still warm.

She sipped her favorite brew and sat on her stool, contemplating the pseudo-Rembrandt and what it meant.

A second forgery by an expert who could imitate two very different painters working in two different media on two types of supports—canvas and copper. Someone who must have experimented in so many ways, with pigments appropriate for each period, tempera vs. oil paint, and the characteristics of different supports.

To distract herself, she unwrapped the latest painting left on her table for cleaning before it was installed in another temporary show about Botticelli and his contemporaries. It was a tempera on panel, from the National Gallery of Art in Washington, D.C. The loan agreement stipulated that Uffizi conservators would clean the painting before displaying in during the month of June, when the new Botticelli installation was supposed to be ready.

Another Madonna and Child. There was that greenish flesh tint again, on both mother and baby—again, a rather adult-looking child. Wait a minute, wasn't that green a little peculiar? It almost glowed where the Madonna's forehead overlapped with the greenish background pillars, and the color was even odder on the drapery next to the child's head.

With a sinking feeling that was becoming all too familiar, Flora fetched her screwdriver and loosened the second frame. Fifteen minutes with her strongest magnifiers told her she had another forgery on her hands. Her heart began to bang in her chest.

She sat down again on her chair, sipping lukewarm coffee and trying to organize her thoughts while she waited for Armani.

Vittorio would have to switch his focus to the murder while assigning others to keep searching for the thief, or thieves, of the original paintings.

She, Flora, was determined to find the forger. A master painter who had carefully experimented on *three* supports: canvas, copper, and wooden panel. He might not be as much of a criminal, in the minds of law enforcement as a thief or a murderer, but to Flora he was definitely someone who must be caught and stopped.

She had to admit, she admired the forger's ability to copy other masters so exactly that most art experts—curators and collectors—were deceived. And his works were proudly hung in one of the most famous art galleries in the world.

Flora just had to meet that guy.

Twenty-three

Flora and Federico approached the lion's den with trepidation. Romano's secretary, Marisa Giusti, warned them he was in a foul mood. The director had just had an unpleasant encounter with the head of the Ministry of Culture about the Uffizi's lack of vigilance in curating Florence's art heritage. Romano had been accused of running a loose ship staffed with imbeciles.

"I hope you have good news for him," Marisa said.

"I wish that were true," said Flora heavily.

She entered Romano's office bearing her notes and cell phone photos. Armani followed her.

"What, both of you? What is this about?" snarled Romano without asking them to sit.

Federico held a chair for Flora and sat next to her. "*Signorina* Garibaldi has identified two more likely forgeries. Unfortunately, they are both loans that have been at the Uffizi for over three months."

"*Dio mio*! I am getting tired of this! Which paintings?"

Flora showed him her photos, notes, and a diagram she'd made of the forger's consistent marks on the edges of the paintings, all hidden when the works were inside their frames.

Romano's naturally swarthy skin darkened until Flora feared

he'd have old-fashioned apoplexy...now known as a heart attack...on the spot.

He growled at her. "How can a slip of a girl be so sure she is right about something so incredibly controversial?"

"I may be wrong. Pigment analysis will prove my suspicions. But I am struck by the similarities in odd colors and painters' marks that are exactly like the first Botticelli, the one we now know to be a forgery." Flora drew herself up. "I may be a small woman, *Dottore*, but I believe my training can compete with any of your other conservators in terms of both technical skill and art historical understanding."

Wow! Did I really say that? If my mamma could hear me now!

Romano stood. "Young lady, I agree your training is okay—for an American. That does not mean you are right."

Flora kept her mouth shut, although she badly wanted to retort, "I am half Italian by blood!"

"But we must have the pigments analyzed, sir," Armani said.

"Oh, all right! We'll do it. Now get out, both of you. I need to make some phone calls."

Flora and Armani left the room with indecent speed.

In the hallway, Federico put a gentle hand on Flora's arm.

"Brava, *signorina*! You stood your ground. I applaud you."

Twenty-four

An exhausted Flora walked home in a misty rain. She knew her fatigue was more emotional than physical. She felt like her feelings had been pulverized by a meat tenderizer.

Romano was such a bully. Despite Armani's presence, the director had treated her as if everything were her fault. Again, he questioned her credentials, her physical stature, and her nationality.

Back inside her chilly apartment, Flora changed into sweat pants and slippers. While she consumed a restorative glass of merlot and cold, leftover pizza, her unhappy thoughts chased each other through her brain.

The director thinks I'm an idiot. A poorly-trained idiot.

My boss in Rome will never send me on another out-of-town assignment.

I can't stand this job another minute.

She rose from the table and paced the apartment, her mood spiraling downward. After tripping over the cat for the second time, Flora told herself to calm down and find a distraction, something more absorbing than a movie stored on her laptop.

The maps. They would take her mind to another place. She spread her copies from the museum library out on her kitchen table and added the modern tourist map of the Uffizi.

Gattino promptly jumped up on the table and sat on the most colorful map, the tourist handout. After patting him until he purred, she moved him to the floor and opened some cat food to buy herself a little cat-free time.

Back to her puzzle. Since she had maps from different periods of the Uffizi's history, sorting out her hoard was tricky.

The first thing she noticed was that half the images were upside down, with north at the bottom of each page. She realigned everything so north was always up. Then some of the map labels were upside down. Worse, the print from her copies was often too small or faint to read. She fetched an extra magnifying glass from her bedroom.

Okay, that looks like a second-floor plan. At least living in Italy had made her think like a European: the second floor became the third floor in an American building. Ground floor meant the one with street access, and the first floor was above that one. At the Uffizi, the ground floor housed the entrance and the bookstore/gift shop, the first floor held Prints and Drawings, office and storage space, and the second floor contained the primary art galleries and the director's suite.

She separated her maps—the ones that were labeled—into piles for each floor.

But some of the Italian labels for first floor said *piano nobile* instead of *piano primo*. Noble floor? Most used floor? She looked it up, suspecting a Renaissance term. Yes, it was: also known as the *bel étage* in French. In a wealthy man's home, it was most elegantly decorated floor, used for entertaining important visitors. This floor sat above the noise and smells of the streets. The top story was usually reserved for more intimate spaces, such as family bedrooms.

Flora remembered a section called a mezzanine, which was supposed to be a half-floor between the ground floor and the first floor. Had she ever been on that level? She didn't think so, and only a couple of maps showed that label at all, without any indication of how the rooms were used.

Gattino reappeared and lay on as many papers as his sturdy little body could cover. She deposited him on the floor and nudged him away with her foot.

She stared at her piles. Okay, which were the oldest maps? The modern tourist map came in handy here, except that it didn't show all the rooms on each floor, but only the ones included in the public tour. A guide had told her this map was printed about two years ago.

Flora compared the tourist maps to the other maps she'd acquired from websites and older publications. Selecting the first floor map that looked like the most current, she labeled the sections she recognized (the offices, conservation lab, tourist entrance, staff entrance, Grand Staircase). There were still plenty of spaces labeled "not in use."

She jotted a note in the margins: who had the keys to those unused rooms?

What about the second floor? The tourist map reminded her that the most important galleries were on that level, with the best-known paintings of the Renaissance and earlier periods. The west side of the building jutted out, so it faced the Ponte Vecchio and ran along the Chasso dei Baroncelli. Some of those rooms were labeled "storage." Others some were marked "offices" or "unused."

The cat jumped on the table again and butted her shoulder. Flora grabbed him and settled him in her lap. She stroked his soft fur and was rewarded with a rumbling purr, quite loud for such a small body.

So many places to hide things! But hiding something as large as the Botticelli would be difficult—unless, of course, the canvas had been removed from the frame and rolled up.

Her head began to ache. Considering how late it was, coffee would be a mistake, but a glass of wine might fit the bill. One glass would clarify her thinking…more than that would just make her sleepy. She dumped the cat, poured a glass of pinot grigio, and returned to her seat. Gattino jumped back in her lap and curled himself into a ball.

Flora sipped her wine, studying the map. Suddenly she noticed a junction between the northern end of the east wing of the Uffizi and the Palazzo Vecchio. It appeared to be a short corridor, well above street level. Now that was interesting. Was that connection open all the time? Open intermittently? Or was the overpass closed to the public and just used for storage?

She made a few more notes and then discovered her head was drooping toward the table. Her phone said it was after twenty-three hundred; Vittorio would arrive any time.

Flora stacked her papers and rose, dumping poor Gattino on the floor. She opened a bottle of red wine for Vittorio and surveyed the fridge for snacks.

~ * ~

It was closer to midnight by the time he arrived.

Vittorio gave Flora a big hug and patted the cat, who leaned against his master and purred.

Flora gave him a dark look. He could hear her thinking, "why do all my cats always like men best?"

He dumped his bags in the bedroom and accepted a glass of wine from Flora. She looked slightly disheveled and sleepy, but the gleam in her brown eyes said she was up to something.

"What's that stack of papers you have there?" he asked.

"I'll tell you later. I want to hear your news first."

Vittorio pushed his chair back from the table and sipped the wine. Then he put his glass down and ran a finger around the rim. The glass obligingly emitted a shrill note.

Flora matched his gesture, getting a different note since her glass had less wine in it. "Remember that musician in Prague, the one on the bridge?"

"The one who played Bach on a wine-glass harp." The memory made him smile until his mind returned to what he'd decided in the taxi. "I'm going to tell you what Esposito found before I left for Rome. I'm breaking departmental protocol—again—but I want your opinion. One of Esposito's assistants identified the name of a known antiquities smuggler on the Uffizi's visitor list from exactly a month ago. We're trying to trace his movements after he was in the Uffizi to figure out if he took the authentic Botticelli out of the museum and sold it to someone else."

Flora refilled her own wine from a bottle in the fridge, taking her time. "I'm guessing you won't tell me the name of the smuggler."

"No, better if I don't."

"Well, my first question is, how did he get the painting out of the building with umpteen guards and an alarm system?"

"We have no idea, but our assumption is that it happened when the security system was turned off and the guards not in attendance."

Flora thought about it. "Perhaps sneaking out of the Uffizi would be easier at the beginning or end of the day, when only staff is present. But there is a single guard posted at the staff entrance when we go in and out."

"What about the middle of the night? We've discovered that there are a few guards taking turns protecting the place every evening." He didn't mention that his team was also checking ventilation ducts as a possible means of hidden travel through the museum.

She stared at him. "Could be, I don't know since I've never worked there at night. But here's my second question. Is the authentic Botticelli still in the country? If it remained in Italy, your Art Squad probably has a list of likely buyers. But if the painting was sold to someone in America or Australia, it will take a lot longer because you'll have to consult police units in other countries."

"Right so far."

Flora pushed the open bottle of red wine closer to Vittorio. "Are you hungry? I've got cheese and melon."

"I'd love some cheese."

She fetched an Asiago and a Fontina from the fridge along with a hunk of crusty bread and two plates and set them on the table. Vittorio reached into the mug where she kept silverware and pulled out a knife.

Flora sat again and continued her musing out loud. She was fully aware that Vittorio had already considered much of what she was saying, but he'd told her she was a great sounding board. He found it useful to review different scenarios with someone outside the police. "If the painting is now in the hands of a private collector, it might never be recovered. You've told me some of the wealthiest collectors just want to own valuable art...they get a thrill from keeping it in private galleries that only a trusted few ever see."

"True enough. That's why our best chance at recovery is when the artwork is in transit from one owner to another. Not a month or weeks after the original sale, replacement, or theft. Not when the trail is stone cold."

"You mean like other crimes, such as murder. The first forty-eight hours is crucial."

"Exactly. The physical evidence is fresh, and there's less chance of contaminating the crime scene if police get in there before other people tramp all over it." He looked at Flora's faraway expression. "What are you thinking about now?"

"That art theft is *your* job. I'm more interested in who did the forgeries and how he or she made the swaps with the original paintings. I bet it was done in stages, using convenient closets or storerooms to stash the forged painting until it could be switched with the real one. The authentic painting may have been moved out of the building the same way—in stages."

Bernini considered this. "You mean, you carry one painting into one part of the museum, you hear a guard coming, and then you hide it temporarily for later retrieval?"

She arched one brown eyebrow. "The best place to hide a painting is in painting storage, mixed in with other paintings in a storeroom. Have you seen ours? Racks and racks of paintings. Or you could hide it in plain sight, with other large paintings stacked against a wall in a gallery where an exhibition is in preparation."

"That Botticelli isn't small."

"Take it out of the frame, roll it up, and stash it inside another rolled up painting of the same size." She smiled evilly.

Bernini shook his head in admiration. "I see how working with paintings all the time provides you with insight on how to transport them."

She nodded. "And if you wanted to hide a painting for a short period so someone else could pick it up, what better way than concealing it with similar objects? You'd have to be very careful, though, to make sure the wrong person didn't make the pick-up."

He took another swallow of wine, rolling it around in his mouth as he considered the implications. "What you've just said could be especially pertinent if two or more people are involved in the painting swap and—"

"And at least one of them works inside the museum," she finished. "So, here's what I've been doing. I'm comparing plans of the Uffizi from different restoration phases over the past ten years or so, looking for all the possible hiding spaces."

"Show me."

Flora moved the food and wine from the table and set the stack of maps between them. "I've only just begun while I was waiting for you to come home. It will take hours more to make sense of it all…"

Half an hour later, Bernini sat back in his chair. "I'd assign someone to work with you, but we're short-staffed."

"Let me work on it and keep you updated every night." She waggled her eyelashes suggestively.

"Your talents are wasted in conservation. You'd make a good spy."

"I'm already a spy—working for you," she said smugly. "Hey, I'm getting sleepy. Time for bed."

"Let's shut the door against Gattino tonight. I want you all to myself."

Twenty-five

Rays of sunshine filtered through the blind. Of course, the weather had improved, now that it was a work day again instead of the weekend. Bernini looked at his phone: six-thirty a.m. He rose, dressed, and started the coffee while making a mental plan of the day and setting his priorities for the investigation.

First order of business: speak with Lorenzo Grandesso of the State Police as soon as possible. He poured coffee into a travel mug and gathered up his briefcase and phone. He peeked in at Flora, still asleep with Gattino on the pillow next to her head. She looked adorable and delicate—vulnerable. He blew a kiss at her sleeping form and let himself quietly out of the apartment.

There was really no time of day or night in Florence without traffic, but at this hour the number of motorcycles and trucks had not yet peaked and the number of cars clogging the narrow streets hardly impeded him. Most people preferred to walk to work, avoiding the problem of finding legal parking. Bernini was privileged—he had a driver at his beck and call day or night—but he often chose to walk. Today, he knew this early morning brisk walk was likely the only exercise he'd get that day.

He arrived at the Carabinieri station at seven-fifteen, meeting Esposito on the stairs.

Bernini asked for an update and then said, "So where is Grandesso?"

"We have a meeting scheduled with him at eight."

"Good. I have just a few questions for him."

"I bet you do, boss."

They entered the coffee room, a mere closet with a coffee machine, a tiny sink, and a stack of cups perched precariously on a chair. Bernini refilled his travel mug with hot brew and a little sugar to kick himself into high gear. Esposito filled his water bottle at the sink.

"Okay," muttered Bernini. "Ready as I'm going to be."

Esposito grinned. They walked down the hall to the conference room. Inside, a huge table perched on decorative bowed legs. A motley collection of chairs was half-filled with Carabinieri from both Rome and Florence and the local Polizia di Stato. *Ispettore* Lorenzo Grandesso entered right after Bernini.

Bernini looked at the face of his long-term rival. The creases in his forehead and the redness of his eyes spoke of a sleepless night and intense grief for his murdered nephew, Davide.

"I am so sorry for your loss," said Bernini simply.

Grandesso stared hard, as if to make sure of Bernini's sincerity.

"*Grazie, Capitano*," he replied in a gravelly voice. "My sister, his mother, is devastated. I will get the bastard who did this, if it is the last thing I ever do."

"You will have our help, of course," Bernini said.

"Huh!" snorted Grandesso, just as the head of the Florence Carabinieri, Colonel Innocenti, entered the room.

Everyone sat. After brief introductions all around, Innocenti took over. "I want to hear first from Grandesso about this undercover operation to monitor the construction team inside the Uffizi."

"Sir, the operation is not just inside the Uffizi, it is all over Florence." Grandesso explained how his men had been watching workers on several projects at both public and private locations, focusing on electricians and plumbers who appeared to be taking shortcuts and using substandard materials. "Someone at the top is directing them to cut corners and save money. We just haven't figured out who it is."

Bernini asked, "Have you investigated the family connections of each of the workers?"

Grandesso gave him a quelling look. "Naturally, we are studying all possible avenues. But this takes time, as I am sure you have learned down south." His tone of voice was lofty and faintly accusatory.

Bernini decided to stay silent and soak up information passively. He stared at a mug half full of stale coffee and sour milk next to a pile of pastry crumbs. Such a familiar sight...the bane of every police station he'd ever been in...but today it made him feel nauseous.

Innocenti proceeded to grill Grandesso on exactly what he planned to do to identify the key players in the corruption scheme.

"I gather your nephew Davide was your inside man at the Uffizi. Do you have other undercover people?"

"Not yet. We are short on manpower, as always. I must identify people who will fit in because they have construction skills, or can be security guards. Being a guard is better because you can go everywhere without restriction."

"I can assign you two more men from the Carabinieri, if you wish," said Innocenti.

Bernini watched as Grandesso considered this less than welcome offer. Each officer preferred to use his own men. The *Ispettore* liked complete control over his operations; he was unlikely to accept men he didn't know well.

"Let me have a few more days, sir. I have a couple of young men I can bring in from just outside Florence whom I've worked with before."

Bernini grimaced as he remembered when he was one of those "young men" on call for both Grandesso and a tyrannical Sienese boss who changed his mind frequently. Like that first boss, Grandesso was a micro-manager, unable to trust anyone to do the job without his personal interference. His behavior drove his subordinates crazy and created bottlenecks of people waiting for approval before acting.

Innocenti turned to Bernini. "Now, I'd like to hear how the murder investigation proceeds. And are you convinced the murder took place because of the Botticelli painting swap?"

"Yes, sir, I do think the murder is related to the theft of the original painting and replacement by an expert forgery. As usual, there's big money involved, and that provides a powerful motive."

Bernini summarized his progress—or rather lack thereof—and made his case for Grandesso postponing his investigation and stepping aside so the Carabinieri could move freely and make decisions quickly without informing Grandesso about every move. He turned to his rival and bowed slightly. "Naturally, if we discover anything that reflects on the corruption case, we will inform you immediately."

Grandesso, predictably, protested. "I will not have my operation compromised or sidelined by an outsider! And I have the right to stay fully informed about any investigation in my jurisdiction!"

Innocenti snapped, "Actually, you don't, Grandesso. I, as your superior, am the one who will be fully informed about both operations on a daily basis." He glared at both men. "There is no reason why both investigations cannot proceed at the same time, but you, Grandesso, will cooperate fully with Bernini and give him the space and any assistance he requires. Unless the situation changes, the murder and theft investigation take precedence over the corruption scheme, and Bernini reports only to me." Innocenti rose and strode out of the room.

Bernini and Esposito exited as quickly as they could, leaving a fuming Grandesso muttering to his sidekick and casting murderous glances at the Roman duo.

Be careful what you wish for, thought Bernini. He wanted a free hand to control his operation, yes, but was the price...making a mortal enemy out of Grandesso...worth it?

Twenty-six

Flora returned from a coffee break with her mind full of plans for chasing down more maps and exploring the less accessible parts of the museum. She bet she'd find plenty of places where one or two people could hide paintings temporarily while they were being swapped with forgeries.

As she turned into the west wing of the ground floor, she saw a couple at the far end of the hall kissing near the temporary office of the Carabinieri. Then she gasped. The man was Vittorio.

The woman was a slender dark woman—similar in build to Flora herself—with her arms wrapped tightly around Vittorio's back.

Vittorio raised his head and saw her. He spoke to the woman, and they both disappeared into the police headquarters.

Too upset to follow him, Flora ducked into the lab with her mind blazing.

How could he? She and Vittorio were living together, and he'd talked about marriage at least twice. She'd put him off because she wasn't ready yet, but that was no excuse for this kind of behavior!

Who was the woman? It sure looked like they knew each other from sometime in the past. But when?

I can't bear this...not now...not with so many other things to think about.

Flora slumped at her worktable, wondering how she could possibly get anything done for what remained of the afternoon.

Alessandro Ferrari usually paid no attention to Flora. Now, he looked up from his table and quirked an eyebrow. "Your face is so white…are you sick?"

"No, I'm not sick. Just got things on my mind."

She shifted her chair closer to her work table so Alessandro couldn't see her face. There was nothing she could do until both she and Vittorio got home, so Flora determined to pull herself together.

She chose the most demanding job she could think of…preparing a conservation report on the Rembrandt forgery. Never mind that she'd have to edit it the next day, when her mind might be calmer.

Half an hour later, she gave up writing the report as a lost cause. What could she do that would satisfy her desire to destroy something?

Her gaze fell on a picture frame that needed new gesso and a reapplication of gold leaf.

First, the old gesso must come off. Seizing a scalpel, she chipped away at it. As she chipped, shedding minute flakes of white and gold on the table, a little refrain haunted her.

Bastard, bastard, bastard…

Flora's work was interrupted by a gentle hand on her shoulder. Vittorio had entered the lab without her even noticing. When had he become so soft-footed?

"*Cara*, let's step outside for a moment." He spoke softly so Alessandro would not overhear him.

Don't "cara" me!

She led the way into the hall and faced him, bristling. "Who was that woman?"

"Her name is Donatella Volpe. She's a *carabiniere* attached to the Florence division and just assigned to this case—you know we need more officers now that we've had a murder."

"But you knew her already."

"Yes. We dated for about six months before I met you."

"How long was that before we met?"

"Ah…we were dating at the beginning of the Siena case. I broke up with her when I fell in love with you."

She chewed on this information. "Clearly it's not over. Otherwise, how why would you both take a chance like that in your workplace when anyone—including me—could see you?"

Vittorio said gently, "Flora, she grabbed me before I knew what she was up to. I was more kissed against than kissing."

Flora remembered that her arms were wrapped around him, not the other way around. This Donatella had imprisoned Vittorio's arms against his sides. She relaxed slightly. "Looked like a long, deep kiss to me."

He sighed. "Right after she kissed me, I told her I was as good as engaged to you, and that we've been living together for months."

"How did she take that?"

"Donatella is not stupid. She nodded and said she'd behave in the future."

I must meet this woman and see for myself what she's like, if I can trust her.

Flora felt her blood pressure subside. "I guess we both have pasts we haven't talked about much. I just didn't expect any of it to catch up with us here."

Vittorio took both her hands. "Flora, I promise you, I'll keep it professional with Donatella. If she causes trouble, I'll threaten her with removal from the case. I have the authority to do that. She'd hate being dismissed because she loves anything connected with the big art museums. She almost became an art curator before she joined the carabinieri."

Hmm, that's interesting. But I don't want to have anything more in common with her!

Vittorio pulled out his cell and glanced at the time. "*Cara*, I have a meeting in ten minutes. We'll talk more this evening, okay?"

"Okay. I'll try not to be grumpy, but it was a shock to see you that way—"

"I know. I'd be the same." He smiled. "No, I'd be much worse. If I saw you in someone else's arms, I'd be ready to punch the guy first and ask questions later."

Flora gave him a watery smile and went back to work.

Twenty-seven

Late that afternoon, Bernini met with his sidekick, Esposito, in the windowless room they were using as a temporary office at the Uffizi. Esposito revisited the question Bernini had raised during the larger meeting. "Boss, do you really think the murder of Davide Grandesso is connected with art theft rather than the shoddy construction operation?"

"I'm not sure. Davide was a security guard, so he had access to locked rooms that could be used for storing substandard construction materials."

He shoved his fingers through his hair. "Suppose Grandesso Junior observed something he shouldn't have, such as a transaction between another guard and a construction worker who has connections to a crime boss outside the museum. That could provide a motive for murder."

Esposito pulled out his notebook and scribbled a note. "Or, Davide stumbled upon art thieves moving an original painting out of the museum. A successful sale of a Botticelli or a Rembrandt to a private collection would generate a lot more instant cash than any savings on construction materials. Especially since we know how long it takes for invoices to be paid around here."

"Unless we discover that the same man is running both the art thefts and the construction racket, we have to focus on the murder of

Davide Grandesso…and let the state police deal with the corruption scandal. One thing that occurred to me…the construction workers have complete freedom of movement in the parts of the Uffizi where they are working. And, because they bring in materials from the outside to build stairs and bathrooms, they have all kinds of packing materials that someone could swipe and use for concealing a painting and then carrying it out of the museum."

Esposito lit up. "Maybe they used PVC pipes to carry unframed paintings! And that thief doesn't have to be a construction worker. It could be a staff member from the museum."

"Or even a member of the public, an outsider who visits often enough to know his way around."

They looked at each other glumly.

Bernini pulled out his maps of the museum, some copied from Flora's trove. "We need to make a new list of all the possible ways in and out of the museum that could be used both during open hours and when the museum is closed to the public."

"At least we can eliminate the HVAC system now."

"Yeah. Only children or midgets could crawl through those tunnels, and I refuse to believe our art thieves are using kids. The only possible access was through the gift shop, and it goes nowhere inside the secure part of the museum."

"Let's leave this mausoleum and walk back to the main Carabinieri office. I have so many questions buzzing through my head I can't think straight. Maybe fresh air will help."

Twenty-eight

The next day, while Bernini struggled to disentangle the Carabinieri operation from the clutches of the state police, Flora plowed on through the treatment of her assigned paintings. The only excitement was a message from Giulia: "Pigment tests on other two paintings shows similar composition of green paint to first Botticelli. Verdict: forgeries."

Later that evening after supper, she found a pocket of time to resume her study of the Uffizi maps. Vittorio remained at work and Gattino slept on the end of the table. Flora dumped her dishes in the sink and gathered up her stash of papers, spreading them out as the sinking sun dyed the shutters orange and russet. A gentle breeze—a nice change from the frigid gusts that had accompanied the recent rains—wafted in through the slightly raised window.

She had gained one key nugget of information: the raised walkway between the Palazzo Vecchio to the north and the Uffizi was the first segment of the famous "Prince's Corridor," also known as the "Vasari Corridor" after the architect who created it in 1565. The passageway, commissioned by Cosimo de Medici for his son's wedding, allowed the nobility to pass unseen and undisturbed between the Palazzo Vecchio, south through the Uffizi, west along the Arno River, and then south across the river and all the way to the Palazzo Pitti.

Lined with some of the most important extant self-portraits of famous artists, the Corridor boasted numerous windows giving spectacular views of the Arno and the center of Florence. The portion over the Ponte Vecchio, the old bridge, was above the gold-and-silversmiths' shops that had replaced earlier butchers' premises. The Corridor provided a convenient and semi-secret route among the three palaces, one that also protected the nobility from anyone interested in their movements.

And, thought Flora, their noble noses wouldn't encounter any unpleasant odors during their stroll from one palace to the other. Pretty deluxe all around: the early dukes and duchesses also had access to an elegant bathroom with marble and frescoes and a private upper gallery in the Santa Felicità church while inside the tunnel.

Flora opened her laptop and tried to determine whether the Corridor had ever been open to the public. One section was restored and opened in 1973, but most of it was closed. A recent article said the Uffizi management was considering moving the portraits so at least one portion, the short passage between the Palazzo Vecchio and the Uffizi, could be viewed by tourists with a combined ticket to the two iconic buildings.

So, at the moment, both ends of the tunnel were either closed or could be visited only with a tour guide. Flora had two options: sign up for one of the tours and pretend she was an inquisitive American tourist, or make friends with a guard to obtain private access. Taking a public tour would allow her to glimpse the spaces and hear some of the history she already knew—and learn some new tidbits. However, making friends with a guard, especially one of the newer younger ones, would be more valuable. She needed someone who'd let her linger in the off-limits part of the Corridor and peer into any storage spaces.

Flora didn't often use her femininity—at least not at a conscious level—to get what she wanted. But this time, she'd be quite happy to flirt in the quest for information that could help Vittorio.

Which guard? She cast her mind over several men, fastening on Fabio Nero. Younger than she by a few years, a bit bored with his job, susceptible to female charms.

The perfect target.

She smiled and closed her laptop.

Twenty-nine

Her tour was set for two in the afternoon on Thursday. Flora decided to take her lunch break late and eat a sandwich on the fly so no one would ask questions about where she was.

Flora arrived at the inconspicuous locked door on the second floor. The door to the famous corridor was "hidden in plain sight" in a part of the building that tourists passed every day. She remembered her fantasy of the Uffizi as a duchess and smiled. The old lady was lounging around in an old gown today, unconcerned if Flora saw her threadbare places. The Vasari Corridor was the equivalent of her boudoir, to be visited only by trusted intimates.

Fabio Nero arrived from the east end of the Uffizi. His smile charmed her, as did his willingness to give her money's worth, although she wasn't a paying customer. His friend Emilia gave tours of the Vasari for a private tour company, so as Fabio assured Flora, he had heard the tour patter several times and knew his stuff.

"Look up," Fabio said as they started their journey. Flora did, admiring the frescoed and gilded ceiling. The Medicis hadn't skimped on the Uffizi palace; apparently, they'd paid the same attention to their private walkway. She supposed that an honored guest might accompany the family on occasion, so the décor was made to impress.

As they progressed down the flight of stairs that led to the outer corridor along the Arno river—visible from ground level or the other shore—Flora took mental note of a couple of closed doors and odd niches.

"Are there closets along here? Or storage rooms?"

"A few," said Fabio airily. "Emilia never opens them. You are the first to ask. I bet the Medicis had stashes of extra furniture, or carriage cushions behind these doors, or other comforts for their mile plus journey from the Palazzo Vecchio to the Palazzo Pitti."

"Carriage cushions?"

"For the little indoor cart in case the lazy nobles didn't feel like walking. It could only fit two people at a time."

Flora couldn't avoid a gasp of surprise when they reached the private gallery looking down into the Santa Felicità church. A low wall—covered with a tapestry, of course—separated the viewer from the churchgoers below. The height of the wall was nicely judged to prevent the Medicis from falling while providing a place to sit or kneel and see what was going on. She wondered if the chairs they'd sat in were gilded like the ceilings.

On either side of the church, there were closed doors that could lead to storage rooms.

"Where's the private bathroom? I read it has marble and frescoes in it."

"That bathroom was destroyed during World War Two. German bombs, of course. But Hitler had visited the Corridor before the war, and he liked the center arches over the Arno and the panoramic view so much that he spared the Ponte Vecchio from bombing. All the other bridges of Florence were destroyed. Mussolini was the one who enlarged the windows."

"Now we're approaching the medieval tower that the Corridor had to jog around—"

"Because the Mannelli family wouldn't consent to having their property cut in two," interrupted Flora.

"You've been reading up on this, haven't you?" teased Fabio.

"Yes. I find the history of this passageway just fascinating."

He smiled and nodded his agreement. They continued their walk, and Flora spotted two more possible hiding places for one or two paintings: behind a massive armoire and a tall wall niche covered with a curtain. Not good permanent hiding places, she told herself, but rather places were someone moving a painting might temporarily stash it for someone else to pick up. Certainly, having a passageway among three palaces gave any thief in the know multiple access points for coming and going.

If—and this was a big if—he had the necessary keys. Did that mean the thief who stole the Botticelli was a museum staff member? Not if he or she had an accomplice with key privileges. What if—no, she'd postpone this speculation until after the tour. She didn't want to miss anything important.

Flora asked her companion about how many times the Vasari Corridor had been totally closed to visitors. She thought she knew the answer, but her information might be incomplete.

"The Corridor is closed to the public more often than it's open. The part that opens most often is the short section between the Palazzo Vecchio and the Uffizi. The section we're in now has needed repeated renovations over time, especially after the world war. Here, we're only fifty meters or so from the Pitti Palace."

They traversed the rest of the Corridor into the Pitti.

"What's that door? Where does it go?"

"I don't know, and I don't have keys to everything. Some of these little spaces have been unused for centuries."

Interesting.

The guard glanced at his watch.

"You have another shift beginning soon?" she asked.

"Yes, so sorry. In thirty minutes."

"No problem, I've seen what I needed to see." They turned back. "So, how long have you worked here at the Uffizi?"

"Six months."

"And how did you get the job?" Flora gave him a flirtatious look, as if to say it was naturally because of his good looks.

He blushed. "My cousin already worked here. He recommended me. It's usual; I think I have five relatives among the other guards."

Flora stared. That was interesting…a network of relatives guarding the treasures of Florence's most famous art gallery. Were any of them criminally inclined? How far did this nepotism extend?

As they exited the Corridor and Fabio pulled out his keys to lock the door, Chiara bustled up to Flora.

"There you are! I knew you'd be off snooping somewhere you don't belong." She stopped right in front of Flora, invading her personal space. "I saw you yesterday when I stopped to pick up some fresh pasta. You were coming out of an apartment building with that Carabinieri officer. I saw him kiss you. You're not just acquaintances, you're lovers! And you, Flora Garibaldi, are more than a police stooge. You're a spy from the inside out."

Thirty

It wasn'treally any worse than before, Flora thought, as she trudged into work the next morning. No one was talking to her very much since that last meeting with Romano. The difference was that now Chiara—and soon the entire Uffizi staff—would know she and Vittorio were extremely close; they'd be sure she'd tell her lover everything on a daily basis.

Just as she turned the corner into the hallway where the lab was, she ran into Donatella.

The woman smiled at her. "Flora Garibaldi, just the person I wanted to see."

Flora was surprised. What could Donatella want with her?

Donatella looked around. "Can we talk somewhere without being overheard?"

Flora thought a moment. "Painting storage is the best place I can think of for private conversations. No one goes there, unless they need to remove a painting or put one back."

They turned back the way Flora had come, toward the west staircase.

Flora pulled out her ring of keys as they descended the stairs. "You'll like this section. It's half-renovated with state-of-the art moveable grates for hanging paintings and half original eighteenth century shelving. The lighting is terrible."

Donatella nodded. "This whole building is amazing. Such a place of contrasts between old and new." She waited while Flora unlocked the door.

Flora led her to the back of the storage area, where some thoughtful person had placed two chairs. Someone who wanted a little retreat, just as Flora did at times?

Donatella took a seat and looked around. "Great place to hide a painting."

"That's what I told Vittorio. I've been trying to think like a criminal, how I would move an original painting and hide it while waiting for transport and hanging the forgery."

"Bernini told me you are good at that, thinking like a cop. In fact, he tells all of us how helpful you've been in different cases." Donatella smiled again. "You know, you don't need to worry about me with your lover. Our affair is past now."

"But you kissed him. I saw that, and it didn't look like things were over, at least on your side."

"I was trying it on. He's good kisser."

I'm not going to comment on that, thought Flora. I'd have to agree with her!

The two women locked eyes until Donatella changed the subject.

"Actually, I wanted to pick your brain about relationships between the staff and the security guards. We're trying to map out the most likely collaborators."

"Well, the guard I just met talked about how many relatives he has among the other guards, and how he was hired—"

~ * ~

Flora and Donatella had a surprisingly amicable conversation, and Flora decided it was okay to trade some of the information she had gathered in exchange for the other woman's assurance that she was no longer interested in Vittorio.

Now Flora sat at her worktable, wondering how she could

remain productive in the investigation. Even Armani would pull back from being her buddy.

Her mind played over the tour of the Corridor she'd taken. So many interesting spaces. Several promising spaces for hiding paintings in transit—

Then Flora sat bolt upright.

Where was the forger's studio? If the old palace had locked rooms that no one used any more, the forger could work either inside the Uffizi itself, or one of the two connecting buildings. The Vasari Corridor was narrow and full of windows, but she'd seen that locked room just inside the Palazzo Pitti. What if there were other such rooms in the Palazzo Vecchio?

But if the forger had a key to an unused room, someone in one of the three buildings must have given him a key. And that meant—

Vittorio appeared in her doorway. "It's lunchtime. I don't see any of your fellow staff around to notice us fraternizing. How about going out with me to find something delectable?"

She pulled herself together. "Love to, especially since Chiara just busted us and I no longer have to pretend that I don't know you very well," she explained.

"That's kind of a relief. We can collaborate openly now. In fact, I'll tell the other cops you're promoted to be an official consultant. This case is so fraught with pitfalls, I'm past caring what my colleagues think about involving my girlfriend. I need all the help I can get."

Finally, thought Flora with a grin. *He's arrived at the state of mind I wanted for him.*

He led her out of the building into the Piazza della Signoria. "Esposito and I have pretty much eliminated the possibility that someone from the outside murdered Davide Grandesso. It's too hard to get in and out of the Uffizi unless you have a key or a security code. That means we must look closer to home—among the people who work here—to solve these crimes."

"I've been thinking along those lines myself. So has Donatella." She told Vittorio about her recent conversation.

Vittorio's eyebrows shot up. "You've made friends with Donatella? That's good."

"Well, we'll never be best buddies, but I can work with her."

He took Flora's elbow and guided her to a Carabinieri favorite: a little family-owned trattoria on a second floor overlooking the Arno. "You will love this place...the pasta is excellent and so is the roast chicken. They do it with unusual spices plus a truffle balsamic vinegar from Modena."

They entered a crowded but charming space that looked like—and probably was—a former salon or living room. The windows were flung open now that the gentle weather of early May had arrived, and the hanging window boxes overflowed with early flowers. Naturally, there were no screens; this was Italy, after all.

As Flora glanced around the cheerful restaurant and inhaled its savory aromas, her spirits lifted. It was a glorious spring day, and Vittorio was in a good mood despite the negative progress on his case. She too felt relief. She was through with sneaking around pretending to be an undercover spy. Now she could complete her conservation work and help Vittorio openly. It no longer mattered if the museum staff distrusted her. What little information she had gleaned about staff relationships hadn't helped the police as much as she'd hoped. Soon she'd be gone for good, back in Rome where she belonged. But there was still so much she wanted to know about the forger,

Flora said, "Back to what you said about looking closer to home—I agree with that approach. I got to know a young guard named Fabio—you'll be interested in what he had to say." She explained about the network of relatives being hired for security work.

Vittorio did not seem very surprised. "I'm beginning to think the Uffizi will turn out to be another family-run operation with almost every hire being a relative of someone already on the staff. That's the way so many institutions are run all over Italy—especially outside Rome. And that practice goes at least back to the Medicis. Esposito told me if we ran DNA profiles, we'd probably discover that most of the Florentines in charge of things today go straight back to the Medicis."

Flora munched on a piece of bread and thought about that. "I suppose it's really no different where I grew up. Chicago is rife with family networks, especially in politics and government. And the deep South—rural anywhere, actually—has its own family networks that stretch back generations."

Their waiter arrived with plates of steaming pasta adorned with a cream and mushroom sauce—*tortellini alla panna con funghi*—and a half-carafe of white wine. He added pepper and fresh Parmesan cheese to the pasta and departed, smiling.

Vittorio told Flora about the rest of his morning, and the conclusions he and Esposito had reached. "We've been distracted by the art smuggler visiting the museum a month ago. His appearance made us look for an outsider infiltrating the building to remove the original Botticelli. Our sources haven't picked up any rumors of new works for sale coming out of Florence, so you may be correct in your assumption that the painting never left the Uffizi."

"Or that it left the Uffizi, but is still in hidden somewhere within the city of Florence. Let me tell you about the Vasari Corridor." She did, noting with glee how Vittorio's eyebrows rose when she described the useful niches and storage spaces she'd observed on her tour. "I think that corridor is an excellent place to hide paintings, or other artwork on a temporary basis."

"Just like the overpass connecting the Palazzo Vecchio and the Uffizi. We examined that space, but I'll check with Esposito. If anyone searched the Vasari Corridor, he didn't tell me about it." He took a bite of pasta.

Flora omitted her recent speculations about the connecting buildings and her determination to find the forger's studio. Vittorio had enough to worry about, and she wanted some leeway to continue her own explorations. If he knew what she was thinking, he'd try to stop her.

He didn't notice her distraction. "There's another thing we've lost sight of...whether or not the shoddy construction practices and the art theft operations are connected, someone is getting rich. It seems likely to me that it's all one operation."

"Follow the money," replied Flora with a grin.

Just as they finished their pasta, the roast chicken arrived, flanked with sautéed tomatoes, onions, and peas. Flora took one bite and shut her eyes in appreciation. "Yum. You were right about this place. And don't expect much supper after such a meal—we can have an omelet and some salad."

They were silent for a few minutes as they wielded their forks and devoured the wonderful food.

Flora paused and put her fork down. She looked at Vittorio's dark head bent over his plate. "What can I do to help your investigation, now that everyone knows we work closely together and live in the same place?"

He wiped his lips with his napkin. "That's tricky. If you ask personal questions, your colleagues will wonder if you are the one who wants to know the answer, or whether you're reporting everything they say to me. But by just being in the museum, doing your regular activities, you may pick up clues we will miss. Yes, I think that's the right approach...follow your regular routines, but don't talk too much."

Flora made a face. "But I still have keys to all of artifact and painting storage. I can go in and—"

"—You don't get it, do you?" His fork clicked hard on his plate. "I think our art thief and our murderer are two different people, *both* of whom work at the Uffizi. It could be more than two people. That means anything you do out of the ordinary puts you in danger." Vittorio's normally dreamy eyes turned hard and his eyebrows slashed a straight line across his face.

Flora gulped. "You're right, I must be careful."

So, this was what he was like at work! She felt like an over-ambitious young policewoman being chewed out by the boss.

Then a novel thought almost stopped her breath. What if she gave up conservation? What if she trained as a cop, and joined the Carabinieri's Art Squad?

Vittorio would hate it. But she, Flora, would be part of the team for real. Her opinions would be taken seriously, listened to by other members of the squad.

And he could never leave her behind again.

Thirty-one

Bernini disappeared on an errand with Esposito. Flora returned to the museum, taking shortcuts wherever she could. She dodged motorbike riders (often well-dressed young women wearing heels with cell phones glued to their ears) and pedestrians. She turned the collar of her light coat up against a chilly drizzle.

Her mind churned with its new bombshell. Change careers midstream...could she really do it? Yes, but did she really want to? It would completely change her relationship with Vittorio. Her idea of joining all his investigations was pure fantasy. If she joined the Carabinieri, she and Vittorio would be colleagues, but she would be his junior for years. Flora would have to complete basic training and then weasel her way onto the Art Squad. She'd report to other officers—multiple bosses—during that time.

The advantage of conservation was that she usually only had one boss, except for this awful sojourn in Florence. When in Rome, she answered to Ottavia, a boss she liked and respected. Here at the Uffizi, she reported to Giulia, but Giulia was clearly under the thumb of the despicable Romano.

She saw similarities between the two jobs: both conservation and being a detective required intense curiosity, attention to the smallest of details, and stubborn persistence. But in the conservation business, most of her "aha" moments were private insights on how to proceed with a painting restoration, rarely shared with anyone else. Flora relished her contacts with Vittorio in his case-solving mode, and the occasional colleague who thought her opinion worth hearing.

Maybe she could prepare herself better by researching what the training period involved. She wouldn't tell Vittorio she was seriously thinking of this big change until she had more information.

Flora already knew the four divisions of the *Tutela Patrimonio Culturale*: archaeology, antique dealing, fakes, and contemporary art. Her art history and conservation training would make her a great candidate for the Fakes division. But she had never held a gun in her life and had no military training. How much of that would she be required to learn? And how long would it take?

At least I have had that self-defense course, she reflected. But that would cut little ice with the Carabinieri.

Flora turned into the museum, showed her badge to the guard, and made her way to the first floor. Giulia had a cubbyhole off the west corridor, and Flora wanted to chat with her about the next item on her list of paintings to be treated.

The door was slightly ajar.

Flora had one foot in the room and her mouth open to speak when she realized Giulia's position was unusual: slumped to one side.

Then she saw the yellow rope—the sort of rope used for packing crates—twisted around her neck.

Her breath caught in her throat, Flora moved forward so she could see Giulia's face.

Contorted, suffused with blood, eyes bulging.

Flora tried to scream, but all that came out was a croak.

She turned around and ran for the nearest guard station.

~ * ~

Thirty minutes later, Flora sat in the Conservation Lab, a hot cup of tea in front of her and Vittorio by her side. Esposito, showing unusual thoughtfulness, had tipped a little brandy into her mug from a flask he kept hidden in his jacket.

"*Cara,* pull yourself together. I know you're in shock, but we need the details if we're to catch the guy who did this." Vittorio put a comforting hand on her shoulder.

Flora's twisted her clammy hands together. "I can't believe it. I talked to her just this morning, and now this—"

"Tell me what happened. When did you arrive at her office?"

She made it through the interview, her mind in a state of mush. Suddenly, policing didn't look like much fun—even on the Art Squad. And she had liked Giulia—most of the time.

"How well did you know your boss?" asked Esposito.

"Not that well. I know her likes and dislikes in the conservation business and how she thinks about other staff—sort of—but practically nothing about her family."

"Is she married?"

"Yes. Her husband's name is...Mario? Marco...I can't remember." Flora shook in her chair.

Vittorio squeezed her shoulder. "You're doing fine, *cara*, just a few more questions and then I'm sending you home."

"But I don't want to leave! I want to find out what happened—"

"—That will take hours, or days. You need some rest, and Gattino purring on your lap."

Could the purring and kneading of a cat really calm her this time? "Okay. I guess."

The two cops asked a few more questions about Giulia's recent behavior.

"Was she worried about anything in the last several days?"

Flora wrinkled her forehead. "Now that you mention it, she did seem distracted. I'd have to ask her questions twice sometimes to get her attention, though she never told me what was on her mind."

Vittorio called his driver to take her back across the Arno to their apartment.

Thirty-two

Now the stakes were raised. With two dead bodies, the police would change their focus to people working inside the museum.

They would have to be much more careful. The night operations could proceed, but with far more caution. He knew it was his job to come up with a better procedure for moving the paintings in and out of their hiding places. Perhaps some of the transfers could happen during daylight? It would be riskier, but not if the prime mover posed as a construction worker.

Those PVC pipes were so useful, but the Boss preferred not removing paintings from their frames. Men in danger tended to hurry, and that meant a higher risk of damage to each painting. The artwork for sale to the highest bidder had to remain in pristine condition.

Then, he had an idea. What about that little storage room on the mezzanine level, the one none of the staff ever went into? A perfect place to deposit paintings for short periods of time...

His blood boiled as he thought about the intruder—that half-American conservator. Way too nosy, that one. Her interference could bring the whole operation to a halt.

They'd have to do something about her.

Thirty-three

Bernini reflected that he had never seen Flora so shaken. Giulia had been Flora's close associate...someone she knew, not a stranger. The corpse was still warm, so the murder must have happened very recently. He shivered, thinking what a close call it had been. If Flora had entered Giulia's office any sooner, she might have met the criminal before he walked away. Chances were, the man—or woman—was still in the building. Or one of the two connecting buildings, the palaces to the north and south. If only he had more men to conduct a search!

He called Grandesso's office and asked for backup. He told Donatella to walk the length of the Vasari Corridor with another officer and search any and all possible hiding places, but he figured it was already too late. Flora had told him how many exits there were: one into the Palazzo Vecchio, one into the northern part of the Corridor, and at least two south of the Arno.

Bernini waited for the crime scene evidence team at the ground floor entrance. He didn't expect them to find much, especially if the perp had worn gloves. Strangling was quick, deadly, and tended to leave nothing behind except the victim's bodily fluids. Giulia had not been stabbed, or dragged, or any of the other things that could mark the murderer, or leave traces of fabric behind. It was sheer bad luck that the murder weapon was a piece of packing cord that could have been picked up anywhere on the museum's ground level.

He realized the murderer could easily be someone on the museum staff who simply did the deed and then returned to his regular job. Therefore, the Carabinieri's most urgent task was to interview everyone in the building and find out who had been where when.

He found his partner just outside the staff bathroom. "Esposito, you and I will interview the museum staff, and we'll assign our junior officers to deal with construction workers and security guards."

"Right, boss. But you think it was another staff member, don't you?"

"Someone who worked closely with Giulia on a daily basis would be the most likely person to have a motive."

"Unless there's another family relationship we don't know about."

Bernini groaned. "This case has too many tentacles into too many different places. I can feel my hair turning gray as we speak."

~ * ~

A few hours later, Bernini and Esposito admitted defeat. They had interviewed every staff member who had been in the building during the likely time frame of the murder identified by the pathologist. No one had seen a thing, probably because the Uffizi boasted so many walls and contained areas that there was rarely a clear line of sight. Flora had told him that as a student in the United States, she had posed as a "guard" in a fourth-floor campus museum.

"You wouldn't believe how ridiculous it was. We had a staff of only five people. I took my turn sitting at a desk behind some Greek statues, with old-fashioned cases of artifacts all around me that blocked my view of the museum entrance. There was no corridor— walking through the museum was like treading a maze. Someone wearing no shoes could have snuck into the gallery and gotten past me, and I would have seen nothing and heard nothing but the pigeons cooing in the eaves."

Bernini's phone pinged.

"Boss," said Esposito, who sounded breathless. "I found something."

"What?"

"A pair of surgical gloves hidden behind a pillar near the museum entrance."

Thirty-four

Vittorio didn't get home to Flora until after twenty-two-hundred that night.

Flora, after taking a hot shower and a much-needed nap, was awake and sipping wine while staring mindlessly at a movie on her laptop. Gattino perched on her lap. His black ears bent forward as he gazed into his mistress's face, trying to divine why she was so fidgety.

"Hi. How are you?" Vittorio leaned over to kiss her.

She touched his face. "All right. I stopped shaking after I took my shower. I think hot water is the best therapy for almost anything."

"And a little white wine completes the cure?"

Flora could feel her lips stretch sideways, a timid version of her usual full wattage grin.

"I can't believe Giulia's gone. It will be really difficult to finish the conservation work without her, but I'll do my best." She caught his somber look as he sat in the chair opposite her. "Oh, no, you're not going to send me back to Rome!"

"Flora, the killer is almost certainly someone you know. Someone who has watched you snoop around the museum and heard you asking tons of questions. I don't have enough men to assign you a guard—"

"I don't need a guard!" *And I don't want to leave you.* "We could team up, move around the museum in pairs…" She stopped as she realized what he was about to say.

"Except you don't know whom to trust anymore."

"But surely you're not talking about the staff I work with daily. I mean, Alessandro or Francesca or Federico. We're not all friends, but we're colleagues—"

Vittorio shook his head. "It could be. We don't know, do we? And we won't know until we find hard evidence or obtain a confession." He spread his hands. "It all takes time, and I don't want you to be the next dead body while we're trying to nail the culprit, or culprits."

Flora's heart sank into her shoes. She hated to admit that the situation had gotten beyond her. It was way outside her comfort zone. Giulia's murder changed everything.

She looked at Vittorio's eyebrows. They'd descended into that straight slash across his forehead, and his lips, normally relaxed, were tight with worry. His expression was harder, more implacable, than she had ever seen before.

He said his final piece. "You can't stay here. You can't help me anymore, and I can't function as well as I'm supposed to if I'm worried about your safety."

A plaintive mew from Flora's lap showed that Gattino sensed the tension between them, not to mention the lack of food in his bowl.

Flora sighed, a long exhalation of air. "I see your point. I'll head back to Rome, but I need one day—Monday—to clear my desk and wrap up as much of my original assignment as possible. The place will be swarming with your men asking questions. Surely I'll be safe for one day."

Vittorio's eyebrows wavered as he absorbed what she was saying.

"One day, then. I'm booking your train ticket for Rome Tuesday morning."

Thirty-five

It was the darkest, coldest time of night: three a.m. Rain beat on the windows and street lights flickered.

Flora, having given up on sleep, paced the apartment in her bare feet. She didn't want Vittorio to wake up. She didn't want to see his face right now, to view that cast-in-stone expression meaning she had failed to make herself indispensable.

Women and children, retire to safety. Get out of the way so the real work can be done.

She wished, not for the first time, that she were a man and safe from archaic thinking and stupid cultural norms. But then she wouldn't know how delightful being a woman could be.

Flora knew she was overreacting, but she couldn't stop the parade of negative thoughts in her brain. She shook her head vigorously as if that would help dispel the demons.

Nothing happened.

She reached down to pat the cat, who was curled up on the kitchen table—a location he was supposed to avoid but never did. Gattino's softness gave her brief comfort.

Her life had taken a turn for the worse; all her assumptions about her future were wiped out. Could she go back to her conservation job in Rome, pretending nothing had changed?

She was a career woman. If she wasn't happy at work, could she and Vittorio survive as a couple? But if she switched to training as a policewoman, a member of the Carabinieri, what would that do to their relationship? What if she had to do her training in another city? Being separated from Vittorio, even temporarily, could make everything harder.

What about getting married and having kids any time in the next decade?

Flora stopped pacing and sat at the table. She buried her fingers in the cat's fur and stroked him. The cat stretched out his paws, presenting his tummy for stroking, and turned his head upside down with eyes closed.

She shut her eyes, focusing on the sound of purring and the softness of his fur.

It will be okay...it will be okay...go to sleep now.

The purr almost worked its magic. Flora lulled herself as long has her fingers were buried in Gattino's fur. Then a cool draft from the partially opened window chased her back to bed.

She lay awake the rest of the night, pondering her options, not sure if she loved or hated the man next to her.

Thirty-six

It was chilly and gray for most of the weekend. Vittorio spent most of his time at work and Flora walked the streets of Florence, saying goodbye to her favorite places. She paid a last visit to the Academy, where Michelangelo's *David* still made her gasp in wonder that anyone could sculpt something so perfect.

Monday morning finally arrived with a burst of activity. She and Vittorio took the Carabinieri vehicle to the museum to save time and to avoid the rain, now reduced to a drizzle. Having the car nearby also meant Flora could load up the supplies and notes she had brought up from Rome. Vittorio returned to his hunt for clues and the next round of questioning of staff, guards, and construction workers. Flora hurried to her lab and found herself alone.

She inhaled strong coffee as she planned her last day in Florence. First item: finish up two outstanding paintings that needed minor repairs and touch-up. Next, leave notes for the conservator taking over. Flora had no idea who that would be, and her mind skittered over the horrible fact that Giulia would never return.

Don't think about it, she told herself...as if that would change anything, or prevent her mind from tumbling like a clothes dryer.

I'll think about that tomorrow. Ah, that was better: channel Scarlett O'Hara in *Gone with the Wind*.

She worked steadily through the morning, and then decided to pick up a sandwich before beginning the dreary job of packing up the supplies and tools she'd brought from home.

On her way back from the staff lounge and a quick coffee, Flora climbed the stairs to the *secondo piano* to admire the building—the indomitable Old Duchess—one last time. Tall, gorgeous decorated ceilings and gracious exterior windows with pillars separating them. The gilded scrollwork above doorways inside the galleries, the amazing chequerboard floors. She imagined the duchess dressed in her best gown, looking regal and totally in control.

On your way, young woman, and don't you forget how privileged you were to visit the most elegant palace in all of Italy. Not many people spend so much time in my hallowed halls.

She would miss the building, but not the job. Now she had too many memories she'd just as soon forget. As Flora passed Gallery 25, she was startled to see the door to the Vasari Corridor cracked open. She cast a quick look around to make sure she was alone and then nipped inside.

Just in time to see a tall figure wearing a visor and carrying a large, painting-shaped package wrapped in brown paper.

Flora descended the stairs and followed him. He, whoever he was, was far enough ahead of her that he couldn't possibly hear her footsteps as long as she didn't bump into anything.

She traversed the portion of the Corridor on the north bank of the Arno, and then, as the passageway jogged south across the river in a series of small left turns, she closed the gap between them.

When the package slipped in the man's arms, he turned his head toward her for a moment.

Giorgio, the mysterious man she'd met in the museum! What was he doing here?

Flora's heart skipped and her breathing accelerated.

She followed Giorgio into the section of the Vasari Corridor south of the Saint Felicity church. She sped up a little to keep him in sight. Just where the passageway jogged right, Giorgio disappeared behind a wall.

Flora heard a sliding sound. She slowed her pace, turned the corner slowly, and was just in time to see Giorgio descending a ladder into a space below them. Where were they, exactly? There were no windows in this section—how strange. Judging from the tour Flora had taken earlier, she guessed they might be in the Pitti Palace, or the section of corridor just to the north of the palace.

She knelt at the hole in the floor and peered down. A studio, equipped with paints, solvents, brushes, easel—everything an oil painter could desire. Two windows near the ceiling gave him enough light to work, but no view from the outside. She had found the forger's workshop—and the forger.

Flora held her breath as Giorgio unwrapped the brown paper. From where she crouched, it looked like another Rembrandt. She debated whether to descend the ladder and question him.

Suddenly a heavy hand landed on her shoulder.

Thirty-seven

"*Signorina*, you definitely shouldn't be here."

She twisted in the firm grip of the head guard, Mario.

"Oh no, you don't. Giorgio, come help me with *questa puttana picola*."

The blond young man looked up and Flora noticed his face was far less friendly than when she'd first met him. He steadied the ladder and said, "Get down here."

She had no choice but to climb down facing away from Giorgio. Her backside tingled with vulnerability. As she descended, she cast her gaze around the crowded room, soaking up as much detail as she could: worktable, storage shelves, a pile of paintings leaning against the wall, some tube-like forms in the corner—

Mario took the rungs two at a time and jumped down after her. He drew a business-like Beretta out of his pocket and pointed it at Flora's chest. "Now, you bitch-who-always-asks-questions, what the hell are you doing in this place?"

Flora's voice stuck in her throat. "I—I followed Giorgio."

"Why?"

"Because he was carrying a painting and I wanted to see where he took it."

The two men glanced at each other. Mario said, "De Luca, bind her and gag her and put her in the storage closet. I'll figure out how to deal with her later."

De Luca? Wasn't Mario's last name De Luca?

In a very few minutes, Flora's hands were tied behind her and an oily rag stuffed inside her mouth. Despite the horrible smell and bitter taste of the cloth, her mind churned away. So, Giorgio was a De Luca as well? More family connections.

As Flora struggled to loosen the strip of cloth around her hands, she wondered where her cell phone was—it must have fallen out of her pocket when the two men shoved her in the closet. Was it possible they hadn't noticed?

"Look, here's her phone. I'll turn it off so she can't use it."

"Just smash it."

Flora heard a sickening smash of metal.

That was an expensive phone!

Silly to worry about that now when her life was in danger. If these were the men who had committed the first two murders, why hadn't they snuffed her already? She shivered and wrestled harder. The loop felt a little looser around her wrists.

Sweat trickling down her back, she paused to listen to the muttering men.

"…when you forge this painting, it will have to be…"

"I create, I imitate. I do not make forgeries."

"Sure, sure. Just remember—"

"I can't work any faster. It will be ready in…weeks, or more. However long it takes."

"…no, that won't do. The Boss wants you—"

Giorgio was the forger, but who was the Boss?

A new male voice sounded at the top of the ladder. "What's going on down there?"

"An intruder. The little girl from *Roma*, the head cop's girlfriend."

"Where is she now?" The voice came closer as the man descended the ladder, and Flora recognized its owner with a nasty, sinking feeling.

Her boss, Stefano Romano. *Why, that creepy, overbearing man—he was the head of the monster! The leader the ring of thieves, in cahoots with his head guard. Was he the murderer as well, or just the guy who made others do his dirty work?*

The door sprang open and Romano looked at her and sneered. "Huh. I like you better tied up like this. Stupid, interfering bitch."

Flora did her best to look un-cowed and defiant, but she suspected her sweaty face with the dirty gag stuffed in her mouth didn't betray much expression. Except for her eyes.

Romano slammed the door shut, so hard that it bounced slightly open.

Well, she was still mute and motionless, but she could listen.

"How long will it take you, *nipote*?

Nephew! Which man was Romano's nephew?

"At least two weeks." That was Giorgio.

"You must work faster than that! My customer is expecting the original painting before the end of May."

Giorgio sounded surly. "I can't do my best work when I'm rushed. I'll do what I can."

A snort from Romano. "See that you do so, or I may have to reconsider employing you." His voice faded a bit. "And Mario, *nipote mio*, when does our courier arrive?"

Two nephews! But why was the director of the museum involved in such a risky scheme? Romano was independently wealthy. She'd heard his wife's family was one of the richest in the entire region of Florence.

"Next Tuesday, sometime after twenty-one-hundred."

"*Bene*. Now, which of you is going to take care of the girl?"

Mario replied. "I will. But what exactly do you want me to do with her? It's broad daylight."

"Hmm. I'll give you something to drug her so she can't struggle. Then you take her east out of the city after dark—Giorgio, you'd better help him. Then you slip her into the Arno in a deserted spot. The current will take her far away and with luck, no one will find her body for days."

Death by drowning. One of Flora's recurrent nightmares had her struggling in slimy, cold water, her legs entangled in razor-sharp reeds—

She pushed her hands apart with all her might. She felt the cloth give, and one hand slipped out. She whipped the horrible gag out of her mouth and pushed the loop off her other wrist. Slowly, moving without a sound, she centered her legs underneath her and rose to a stand. After her legs stopped wobbling, Flora stepped behind the door so it would cover her temporarily when it opened.

"Do you have the drug with you?" asked Mario.

"No, of course not. I have to fetch it."

She heard the creak of the ladder as someone climbed. The men were leaving.

Listen! Will they turn north, to cross the Arno? Or south to exit the Vasari Corridor inside the Pitti Palace?

The ladder thumped its uneven legs on the floor as another man climbed up. Flora heard the floor panel being dragged back into place. The footsteps receded to the north. Assuming they would go back to the Uffizi, she'd better go to the Carabinieri station or the *Questura*. Which was closer? She couldn't remember.

She waited as long as she could stand it, counting slowly to a hundred.

Safe or not, I'm outta here.

Flora climbed the ladder and placed both hands on the wooden panel above her head. She pushed, but nothing happened. Then, remembering the sliding sound it had made, pushed sideways at the same time she pushed up. The panel moved to one side and she hoisted herself through the opening.

She ran south, toward the exit that must be somewhere ahead in the Pitti Palace.

Flora turned a corner at full speed—and ran right into Giorgio's arms.

Thirty-eight

"Let me go!" Flora wrestled with him. He was awfully strong for someone so skinny.

"Calm down! I will not hurt you. I mean to take you to a place of safety."

She stared at him in astonishment. "Why should you help me? Isn't Romano your uncle as well as your boss?"

"He is my uncle by marriage, yes. But my job is not worth being involved in a murder. I will not help Mario dispose of you. I am a painter, a master artist. I make works for my uncle to sell, but I do not join in his more criminal activities."

Privately, Flora thought this was a fine time to be making such distinctions, but she looked into Giorgio's big blue eyes and believed him.

"I must find Vittorio Bernini."

"Your policeman lover?"

"Yes. Please help me."

"Follow me, this way. I know another way across the Arno where we will not run into the others at the Ponte Vecchio."

They set off at a fast trot, exiting the Pitti Palace at the back of the building. It had rained during her adventure, and the wet cypress trees emitted a refreshing resinous smell. He led her through the palace grounds to a tiny street leading to the Piazza de'Mozzi.

"Giorgio. You are the forger, am I right?"

He turned his curly head toward her with an enchanting smile. "I do not call it forgery. I call it worshipping the masters by imitation."

Flora, as sweaty and dirty as she was from her time in the closet and fast run into Giorgio's arms, snorted in disbelief. "You do understand the Art Squad doesn't see it that way?"

Never mind the museum administration—oh, sorry, her boss was part of it—and the art world.

Giorgio managed to speak calmly while walking with a fast lope that left Flora breathless. "I am an artist, first and foremost. What people do with my works is not my concern. I do not sign my pieces, so is it my fault they are interpreted as a Botticelli or a Van Eyck? I strive to achieve perfection in color and line, and exact pigments for each period. This requires all my concentration."

Flora stayed silent, recognizing the man's head-in-the-sand focus on his art. Truly, he was the perfect patsy; any unscrupulous boss could make him produce masterpieces for sale to the highest bidder. And where was Botticelli's *Birth of Venus* now? And the other two stolen originals? She could hardly wait to reach Vittorio and show him the tubes—perhaps containing rolled-up canvases—she'd seen in the corner of Giorgio's incredibly messy workshop.

They reached the Alle Grazie bridge. Giorgio increased his speed so Flora couldn't keep up with him. But the friendly walls of the Uffizi loomed ahead just to her left, and she knew the closest entrance was on the south side.

By the time Flora crossed the courtyard to the staff door, Giorgio had vanished. She ran along the ground floor, intent on reaching the temporary Carabinieri office at the west end of the building.

Stefano Romano stepped out of the hallway to her right, blocking her way.

Instead of running away, Flora waited for him to run at her.

As Romano reached out his right arm to grab her, Flora seized the arm in both hands and pulled it across her chest and down while pivoting to the side.

He lost his balance and crashed to the floor, face down.

Flora immediately fell knees first onto Romano's back, causing him to grunt with pain. When he recovered his breath, Romano began cursing Flora using some colorful phrases she had never heard before.

A voice sounded behind her. "Why have you attacked your boss? Are you trying to get yourself fired?" Esposito, of course.

Flora panted, "He's the head of the theft-and-forgery operation. And he tried to have me killed."

Vittorio ran up to them. He helped Flora up and pulled her close. "Did you say Romano is our criminal? Explain."

She gave him the short version as Esposito handcuffed Romano. Donatella and another officer arrived, guns drawn, and flanked the prisoner.

Romano spat at Flora, who moved out of the way.

Esposito grinned. "I saw how you took him down, *Signorina*. Not bad!"

"I can't believe that worked. I learned it in self-defense class."

"Classic move, using your opponent's weight and momentum against him," said Esposito.

Vittorio looked stunned. "We'll adjourn to our temporary office so Flora can make a complete statement." A trace of a smile showed. "And while you're at it, you can tell me why you always end up in the middle of our operations."

"Maybe I belong there," Flora said.

His eyes widened. "We'll talk about *that* later."

"*Va bene.*"

Thirty-nine

Colonel Innocenti presided over the Carabinieri and *Polizia di Stato* meeting the next morning. Flora, still a bit pale, sat as close to Vittorio Bernini as she could get without sitting in his lap, or spoiling his image. To her surprise, the other cops welcomed her presence with nods and grins—even Esposito. Did he have a human side after all? Perhaps the judo throw had given her a kind of credibility her brainpower had not? Maybe she could work with these people.

Innocenti nodded at Bernini to present his report while Grandesso glowered from the sidelines. Bernini summarized the early investigation and then told the story of recent days. "Since we shifted our focus to the museum staff, Romano was on our list of suspects, but we had no evidence until yesterday." *Signorina* Garibaldi's misadventure gave us the proof we needed." Bernini cast a warm glance in Flora's direction and all faces turned her way.

He continued. "More than half the people working here are related to Stefano Romano, owe him something, or know a member of his family intimately. It turns out that both Mario, the head guard, and Giorgio, the art forger, are his nephews."

"Has Romano confessed to anything yet?" asked a young policewoman Flora had not met.

"No. We have only begun to question him, and our men are gathering evidence as we speak to put pressure on him by persuading him that we know too much for him to get away with anything."

Esposito chimed in. "Half the construction workers are related to Romano, as well as some of the outside contractors."

Bernini nodded. "The network of family relationships makes it likely that all the crimes—the art thefts, the substitutions of expert forgeries, and the shoddy construction, are all connected."

"That makes sense, but we need a lot more evidence," Grandesso said sourly. "Perhaps now that the murders are solved, you'll permit me to finish my part of the job?"

The colonel spoke. "Yes, of course. Bernini must return to Rome, and you, Grandesso, will be back in charge of the corruption scheme. But what was Romano's motive? Money?"

"Money is assumed to be the motive, although as Flora pointed out, Romano was already rich through his marriage to Adona Rossi. The Rossi family is loaded," Bernini paused.

"I can add to that, boss," said Donatella Volpe. "I've done some checking of Romano's bank records and he is going broke. Too many bad investments and fingers in too many pies. He needed money, and fast." Her eyes glinted at Bernini, but then she smiled at Flora.

Flora smiled back.

Donatella added, "And here's another family connection: the dead woman, Giulia Rossi, was a cousin of Romano's wife Adona."

Bernini nodded. "One more bit of evidence that the whole museum was riddled with nepotism."

"No different from any other Italian organization," commented Esposito. The others responded with chuckles and eye-rolling.

Bernini glanced at his notepad. "Romano refuses to talk until his fancy lawyer shows up, but Mario De Luca is singing loudly. He ran a network of guards including his assistant, Pietro, and their newest hire, Fabio Nero." He turned to Flora. "I'm afraid Fabio gave you away to Mario after he gave you your tour of the Vasari Corridor."

"I was too trusting. I just have to learn to be more suspicious—of everyone," said Flora. This drew a real laugh from the assembled cops.

Bernini grinned. "We've yet to learn who actually committed the murders, but my money's on Mario. He's no longer pretending to be bumbling and disorganized. He comes across as a thoroughly savvy thug."

The meeting wound up shortly after that, with Bernini handing out a few more assignments to clean up loose ends while he and Esposito conducted final interviews with Mario De Luca, his assistant Pietro, and Stefano Romano.

As everyone rose to go about their business, Grandesso actually shook hands with Bernini. Surprised, Bernini said, "*Grazie, Ispettore,* for your cooperation."

Esposito buttonholed Flora.

"I hope you're okay after your ordeal, *Signorina* Garibaldi? You really did awfully well, escaping from that closet and taking care of Romano." She detected a twinkle in his eye she'd never seen. "I hope you'll accept my apology for, ah, being less than gracious to you. You are clearly a big help to the Carabinieri."

Flora laughed. "I forgive you, Esposito. And stop calling me '*Signorina.*' I'm Flora." She looked at Bernini for approval and he nodded. "I'm cooking tonight, Esposito. Why don't you join us for supper?"

"I'd like that. And call me Raffael."

Forty

On the way home, Flora asked. "What about Giulia? Why did she have to die?"

"We don't know yet, but the diary we found in her handbag showed she had a bit of a crush on her boss. I'm guessing Romano thought she was getting too close to his operation and killed—or had her killed—to prevent her coming to us. I'll show it to you—I have a scan of it on my laptop."

"That would explain why she was so preoccupied last week."

He found a parking spot almost in front of the apartment; that had never happened.

They climbed the stairs and entered the hallway, dropping keys and briefcase on the table near the door.

Vittorio said, "You need some wine before you start cooking—and so do I. Let me pour some. Red or white?"

"White. But I need to clean up a bit. Give me a few minutes."

When Flora returned to the kitchen dressed in leggings and a soft tunic, he had pulled out two kinds of salami, bread, cheese, and olives. The chilled pinot grigio awaited her, and she took her glass and sank into her usual chair.

He handed her his laptop and she read Giulia's last diary entry:

I don't know what is going on, but I am beginning to mistrust my boss. Stefano uses me as a messenger girl, delivering verbal orders to some of his guards and construction workers. On the face of it, each one is innocuous: "meet me at seventeen hundred in paintings storage," or "your package is in the usual place." Is he somehow connected with the recent crimes in the museum? If he is, just how gullible does he think I am? He must be very sure of me. I have nothing concrete to show the police...that makes sense if he really is up to something criminal and wants no record of these messages. It would be his word against mine...oh, what shall I do?

Flora sighed as she read her friend's words. Yes, Giulia had become a friend as well as a boss.

Vittorio drew her attention away from his laptop. "Flora, we have some time before Esposito arrives. What did that enigmatic remark of yours mean? When you implied that you belong in the middle of our Carabinieri operations?"

She met his eyes. "I'm thinking of leaving conservation and training to become a Carabinieri officer. I'd like to join the Art Squad when I'm fully qualified."

His jaw dropped. "*Oddio*! I mean, are you serious? Have you thought what that will mean?"

"I've been thinking of nothing else for days. I'm getting sick of lab work, of bending over a big table with toxic fumes in my face, slaving away at paintings. My finished work is only satisfactory if it is undetectable, invisible. Conservation is essentially a solitary pursuit, except for talking with other conservators. We are usually all introverts to a certain extent, people who thrive on working alone.

"The recent events at the Uffizi made me realize I've changed. I'm a bit more of an extrovert now. I'm happier dealing with people, asking questions, moving around the city. Being part of a bigger operation—one that leads to meaningful results for the art world."

Vittorio's face was a study in conflicting emotions. Flora imagined she saw shock, mixed with dismay, and something else she couldn't identify.

He took a big swig of wine and reached for a chunk of salami. He chewed thoughtfully.

"I can't quite wrap my head around this. You, working in the same profession—probably in a different division most of the time—engaged in investigations and house searches. It would change our relationship."

"Of course. But I know of many successful relationships with both people are in the same profession."

"Granted. But in this case, it could be a disaster." His face grew stern. "Much of our work brings us into contact with criminals. You'd be in physical danger—"

"And I haven't been in danger already, assisting you as a civilian?"

He chose to ignore that. "And do you have any idea what real discipline is like? In a military unit—or a police unit of the military—orders are obeyed without question because lives are at stake. You'd have to report to someone who didn't care about your individual wishes but only the health of the people on his team—and the success of the mission. And if you did something without getting permission first, you'd be demoted or otherwise punished."

Flora's heart sank. "I've been thinking about that aspect of police training. When I've done other kinds of training, I have adapted to what was expected of me. I can do that again, if I'm motivated enough."

Vittorio shook his head. "I think this is a crazy idea. You should stick to conservation. You're good at it, you already have the training, and you make decent money."

"But—"

"I don't want to talk about it more tonight—certainly not in front of Esposito. We're both exhausted, and something this serious needs the light of day."

She swallowed. "Okay, you're right. But Vittorio, we do have to talk about this again. Soon."

Forty-one

Flora and Vittorio returned to Rome together after all. Vittorio stayed in touch with the Carabinieri and *Polizia di Stato* in Florence. Lorenzo Grandesso and his team grilled the construction workers and confirmed that Stefano Romano had run both operations, the swapping of original paintings with forgeries and the shoddy construction. Grandesso faxed his report to Vittorio.

Esposito stayed on in Florence to clean up loose ends. One of those loose ends was who had messed up Flora's work station and squirted her paints onto the floor: Francesca, the disgruntled younger conservator. The other loose end was Giorgio, who had disappeared without a trace.

Flora found herself glad for Giorgio. Yes, he had participated in a criminal enterprise, but he was an awfully engaging criminal (he would say artist and imitator) and he *had* rescued Flora from the clutches of the despicable mastermind, Stefano Romano. No doubt Giorgio would re-establish himself in some other city, setting up a new studio and pursuing his peculiar occupation of copying great masters. Perhaps he would turn his talents to something safe, like doing museum-quality reproductions for money.

The memory of Giorgio's face stirred up something forgotten. His blue eyes—that cloud of hair—now she knew why he looked so familiar! Giorgio De Luca looked like the angel in a Botticelli painting.

Ottavia had plenty of work for Flora to do, but those projects did not prevent Flora from ruminating on a career change. During her breaks, she thoroughly investigated the Carabinieri website, especially the recruitment and training page. She discovered that certain civilians with specialized skills could bypass some of the traditional training. Although art conservation was not listed, she thought a case might be made for her. Flora also called the training school in Modena and had a long chat with a recruitment officer. He was quite encouraging and wanted to know when she would apply.

"Soon, but I need to get my family on board with this first," Flora replied.

The officer promised to send her a packet of forms and information by snail mail. Flora gave him the address of her laboratory instead of the apartment. After her last aborted conversation with Vittorio, she wanted to choose a better time to talk with him. She'd wait until she had all the information she needed to make a clear-headed, well-informed choice.

Forty-two

The duchess felt considerable relief as the streams of policemen packed up their equipment and left the museum. Gone were the computers and folding chairs that had no business in her exceptional palace. The construction workers deserted their posts, sent to jail while replacement workers and managers were recruited. She stretched, hearing pops and creaks as the old walls adjusted to steel beams and metal elevators—foreign materials that didn't fit the Renaissance architecture of the original structure. At least the new staircases, still in progress, were designed by experts who appreciated graceful lines and lofty spaces. She thought the Copper Staircase was quite handsome. Distinguished.

There was no way to get rid of all the tourists, though. The duchess supposed they weren't all bad. After all, they came from every country of the world to admire the Uffizi and its treasures. Then they went home and boasted to their friends, who then planned their own trips to Florence.

She preened a little, thinking of how well the new galleries would complement the Medici possessions and the works of famous artists. No other museum in the world could surpass her beauties.

Now, however, the sun was setting, the silly little people hastened toward the exits and it was high time to relax. The duchess rolled over and composed herself for sleep. She smiled as she contemplated how long the Uffizi had lasted, how many years it would still stand.

And after all, scandal made her even more famous. Stolen paintings, expert forgers, criminal construction workers made great subjects for international news. The checkered history of the Uffizi would survive.

And so would she.

Forty-three

Flora's opportunity came in early June, when she and Vittorio were trapped together on an overseas flight to Chicago. They had promised Flora's parents they'd visit as soon as the Florence operation was over. Vittorio would not be able to escape being looked over by a horde of Flora's siblings and aunts and cousins.

Since it was a daytime flight, neither of them was sleepy. The Italian airline served a decent lunch with wine, so Flora figured she'd never have a better chance to get Vittorio's full attention.

"Tell me about what Esposito said yesterday."

Vittorio scraped the last of his pasta out of its aluminum foil compartment. "He gave me a summary of how many Uffizi employees were involved in the paintings swap operation." He looked at her, dark eyebrows raised.

Flora played along. "More that you thought?"

He nodded. "Half the guards. Mario rearranged the guard roster, so only his men were in the museum overnight. Romano also recruited two construction workers—an electrician and a painter—and one curator."

"Not Giulia?"

"No, she was just a patsy, manipulated by Romano. The curator was someone you never met, a guy named Riccardo Lupa. He also worked under Romano, but he was in charge of moving stolen paintings and traveled frequently throughout Europe."

"I guessed Giulia was falling in love with her boss. I remember sensing an energy between them whenever they put their heads together."

"As I told you, her journal confirms she had some romantic feelings. I bet Romano knew of her weakness for him and used it to his own advantage. He made her run all kinds of errands, and later entries in her journal revealed that she knew she was venturing into dubious territory."

"What do you mean?"

"Giulia wrote that Romano asked her to stay late on one occasion to watch the CCTV while the guards 'did something important' for him. She knew there was something fishy going on, but she was scared of Romano at the same time she was in love with him."

"Whew," Flora said. "I don't envy her."

The steward offered them each another little bottle of wine, which Vittorio accepted. Flora asked for fizzy water with ice. She wanted to keep her head clear.

"Vittorio, couldn't we talk more about my desire to retrain for the Carabinieri?"

He made a face. "I guess so. I know you've been broody, and I haven't given you a chance to get it off your chest."

She took a deep breath. "I've read everything I can find about the training options, and I think I might qualify as a technical-logistics officer like civilians who come in permanent service with an external degree in forensic science or pharmacy or engineering."

He listened, sipping his red wine. "If you're right, that would mean you wouldn't need the two years of army training in Modena."

It sounded like Vittorio had been doing a little research of his own!

"I'd need to pass a public examination, though, and since I went to college in the United States, that might take some extra prep."

He looked at her and smiled. "You'd have no trouble with the examination, but you might need to brush up on Italian technical terms."

She grabbed the hand closest to her. "Vittorio, I want to do this. I think I'd be good at it. I'd have to adapt to police discipline—" she smiled as she saw his eyebrows shoot up—"but I think it would be worth it."

He squeezed her hand. "It's true you have the aptitude for this kind of work, and your conservation background would be really useful in the forgery or modern art divisions. My biggest concern would be how to get you enough arms training so you could protect yourself."

She teased him. "Well, I do know a little judo."

He grimaced. "You know that's not enough."

"Actually, I found an announcement of gun training for Technical-Logistics officers who want to accompany regular officers on certain types of operations."

He shook his head, this time in admiration. "I have to admit— you sure know how to research something you're interested in."

Flora played her ace. "I discovered that the old Carabinieri policy that discouraged marriage between officers has been replaced with a more liberal one."

His face lit like the sun. "Did you say marriage?"

"Yes, I'm finally ready to get married. Once I'm fully trained and gainfully employed again, we can figure out when to have kids. That part won't take any more juggling than a conservation career...the pregnancies might even be easier because I'll be in better physical shape as a police woman than as a lab rat."

Vittorio grabbed her shoulders and kissed her soundly, much to the amusement of nearby passengers.

After they disentangled, he quirked an eyebrow at her. "Time to tell the parents we're getting married?"

"Yep, time to tell the parents." She smiled as she looked at the time on her phone. "You have about five hours to brace yourself."

He closed his eyes. "*Oddio*."

Forty-four

Vittorio paced the bedroom. They'd been in Chicago only a few hours, and already he wished he were anywhere else, preferably back in Rome.

"She said you're a typical Italian mamma's boy," teased Flora.

"Why did she say that?"

Flora made a face. "My mamma is not the most tactful person in the world. I think she meant it as a compliment, believe it or not."

Vittorio focused reproachful eyes on her face. "I don't take it that way. It sounds like she believes I have no backbone and no mind of my own, that I am still a boy and not a man."

"Maybe she likes your hair, the way your bangs grow long and floppy."

He threw a pillow at her. Flora ducked and the pillow landed on the floor next to a pinewood bureau.

"Hey! It went okay for a first introduction!"

Vittorio sat down hard on the bed, causing the mattress to buckle and almost tip Flora off the edge. Yes, he was still nervous about meeting the rest of Flora's family, but he was delighted to see his love playful again. Her eyes danced and her voice lilted in a way he hadn't seen for months.

"Uh-huh. I can hardly wait to meet your father." He let a bit of a growl sound in his voice.

Flora chuckled. "My dad is an easy-going man, you'll see."

"Is any man easy-going when he meets his daughter's lover for the first time?" Vittorio lay back on the salmon-colored tufted bedspread. He turned his head sideways to view the skyline of Chicago at sunset. Pretty spectacular, he had to admit. The scenery was different, but the delectable aromas of garlic, tomato, and herbs reminded him of his mother's kitchen.

Flora reclined next to him, her head resting on her propped-up hand. She looked so relaxed. "You face criminals with steely confidence, Italian colleagues with calm, and you're afraid of my parents?"

He turned back from the window, relishing the sight of her seductive pose and mischievous face.

"Actually, they scare me too," Flora said. "Every single time I bring a new person home. Male, female, trans-gender, it doesn't matter. The poor visitor gets the prisoner-intake interview from my mamma and the once-over by my dad. No one is ever good enough to be my friend, let alone my future life partner."

He sat up, smiling. "It's not just me? Do they do the same thing to your brother and sister?"

"Of course."

Vittorio sighed. He still had to get through the next few days without making too much of a fool of himself.

"Flora! Your dad is home. He wants to meet your boyfriend!" Flora's mother called from the kitchen.

Vittorio stood, tucking in his shirt.

Flora grabbed a comb and smoothed down her hair. Vittorio preferred it wild and Medusa-like, but now was not the time for the just-out-of-bed look. He and Flora had momentous news for her parents.

She opened the bedroom door.

They traversed the upstairs hallway and paced sedately down the stairs to the living room.

A tall man with pepper-and-salt hair and a craggy, interesting face awaited them. "Daisy, my flower!" he crowed as he swept Flora into a bear hug.

Then he faced Vittorio with an outstretched hand. "Ian Garibaldi-McDougal. Vittorio, it's good to finally meet you."

"Yes, sir, it's high time." Vittorio took the hand and felt instantly comfortable. Flora's dad was okay.

Then Ian spoiled it. "What are your plans?"

Vittorio gulped. "Ah—."

Flora jumped in. "See the sights of Chicago and meet the relatives. We'll give Vittorio a chance to get used to us."

McDougal grinned.

Vittorio relaxed. "I've never been to Chicago," he admitted. "Or the United States."

"And you've never met the combined Garibaldi-McDougal clan! What an experience you have in store." His eyes twinkled at Vittorio. "Call me Ian. Now, what would you like to drink?" The two men headed in a purposeful way toward the liquor cabinet.

Flora watched their broad backs, observing that Vittorio was shorter than her dad, but no less powerful looking.

A yell from her mother made her head swivel toward the kitchen. "I could use some help out here!"

"Just coming, Mamma!"

When she entered the kitchen, her mother faced her, arms akimbo.

Flora gave her parent a hug, a move calculated to deflect criticism before it began. Silvana Garibaldi felt solid. Her body wasn't plump, just compact and springy with energy. Her dark curls were sprinkled with gray, and her brown eyes snapped with street smarts and avid curiosity.

She started in on her favorite theme. "So, is this Vittorio 'the one'? The one you will marry and have babies with?"

"Mamma! Always the same questions!" Flora said, wrapping the strings of an apron around her waist and stalling for time. She and Vittorio had decided to choose their moment, hopefully when the parents had imbibed some wine, to tell the parents about Flora's career change before they introduced the subject of marriage. "We've only been together about nine months."

"I knew I wanted to marry your father in three weeks."

"I'm not you. Not everyone has the same experience, Mamma."

"You share the same apartment. You must know by now."

Flora kept her gaze on the carrots she was peeling. "My friends live with each other for months, even years, without marrying. I need to be sure we can get along in bad times as well as good ones."

"But until you make the commitment, you can't know how much hard work it takes to stay together! You must have a mortgage together, a child or two. You have no idea!" Silvana Garibaldi shook her head vigorously as she slapped pasta rectangles onto her cutting board. Grabbing a spoon, she placed small amounts of filling on one half of each shape.

Flora finished the carrots and picked up a little bowl of egg white. She brushed it around a filled pasta rectangle, folding and pinching it to seal the edges. She moved on to the next one. The completed ravioli would be boiled and dressed with her mother's signature sauce and dusted with grated parmesan for their first course.

"Mamma, I think we are talking about the same thing…the best way to be sure about choosing a life partner. I think if we agree on work and life balance, on how to spend and save money, on religion and politics, the other stuff will fall into place."

Daughter and mother locked gazes over the filled pasta squares.

Silvana sighed. "Perhaps you are right. I understand that young people do things differently now. But in some ways, it was easier when our parents chose the family, the spouse. We learned to love each other over time."

"You think I should be like Aunt Elena and Uncle Lorenzo? They had an arranged marriage and they fight all the time."

The men strolled into the kitchen.

Vittorio glanced from one woman to the other. "You talk of marriage?"

Ian groaned. "Silvana is always talking about marriage! For her children, her nieces, her friends' children—"

Vittorio's mouth twitched. "Isn't it unusual for a Scotsman to marry an Italian?"

"Not if they love each other," replied Flora's dad.

"Aha! Yours was a love match after all!" Flora enjoyed teasing her parents.

Silvana threw a potholder at her husband. "If you can call such foolishness a love match!"

Ian caught the pot holder. "Well, you eloped with me, didn't you, Silvana?"

Flora turned on her mother. "Mamma, you didn't! After all this time, letting me believe you had a traditional wedding, all arranged by your papa!"

Silvana busied herself at the stove. She stirred her marinara sauce with unusual vigor. "It wasn't my idea. It was all Ian's!"

Her husband burst out laughing. "Now that's rich! It was *your* idea to elope, because you couldn't face your papa and tell him you wanted to marry a foreigner! And here you are, twenty-five years later, laying down the law about marriage to anyone who will listen!"

"I only want the best for my little girl," she muttered.

Flora was amazed. She'd never seen her proud mamma look sheepish. And her parents had just handed her the perfect ammunition to explain her own choices.

At this fascinating moment, Vittorio's cell phone buzzed. He looked at the tiny screen, frowning.

"*Pronto.*"

Little fingers of foreboding tapped on Flora's spine. She watched Vittorio's face and saw his dark eyebrows draw together.

He turned away from Flora and her parents.

Silvana raised her eyebrows at Flora.

"It must be the Carabinieri," whispered Flora.

Vittorio pocketed his phone and squared his shoulders before turning to face them.

"I have to return to Rome."

"When?" Flora's lips felt stiff.

"Tomorrow. If I can get a flight."

"But you just got here! You're going to meet the whole family tomorrow night!" cried Flora's mother.

Flora watched Vittorio's face harden into his official Carabinieri mask.

"It's not a choice, *Signora*. I must go when my job demands it. There's been a major art theft in Naples, with two museum guards murdered. I must be on the next plane out of Chicago." His gaze fixed on Flora, begging her to understand.

"*Merda*," she said, so softly that only Vittorio could hear her. It would always be like this. Not just for Vittorio—for Flora, too.

Flora's parents wore identical scowls of dismay. She could see them thinking *this man will always take our daughter away*—

Vittorio relaxed his face into its usual appealing mode. "Let me make a couple of phone calls. I'm pretty sure most flights back to Italy are in the late afternoon, so we'll have this evening and a good chunk of tomorrow." He moved out of the kitchen.

"Mamma, at least we're here tonight. Let's make the best of it," Flora pleaded.

"Oh, all right. We will still have a good meal." Her mother turned back to the stove.

Her father was more accommodating. "Of course, we are disappointed he has to leave so soon. But you can stay the full week, can't you, Flora?"

"Yes of course, Papa."

"Let me pour you a glass of wine."

Vittorio returned, pocketing his phone. "I'm all set. I leave tomorrow at sixteen-thirty—I mean, four-thirty your time." He looked at the counter where Flora had spread out salad fixings. "Want me to chop something?"

Silvana smiled. "A man who is useful in the kitchen! Will wonders never cease!"

"I can cook a mean omelet," boasted Vittorio.

"*Va bene*," she said with a mischievous grin. "You may cook breakfast tomorrow morning."

Ian said, "You walked into that one!"

Flora seized the opportunity. "His cooking skills will come in handy while I'm retraining."

Her mother turned. "What!"

"I'm going to join the Art Squad of the Carabinieri and put my conservation skills to practical use catching forgers."

"What? Are you crazy? *Dio mio*, a daughter of mine a policewoman—" She was launched and spitting fire.

Vittorio waited until Silvana stopped to catch her breath and said, "*Signora,* it's not so crazy. Flora will be a special kind of officer, more a consultant than an ordinary cop. Her work will be very interesting, and her weapons training—"

"Weapons? But she'll be in danger!"

Flora said calmly, "Mamma, I've been in danger before and the police have protected me. I'll actually be safer if I carry my own weapon—one I know how to use."

Ian said mildly, "Is it what you really want to do, Daisy?"

She turned to her father eagerly. "It is. I want to be more useful to the art world than I've been up until now, hidden away in a laboratory. I prefer the kinds of interaction I have when I've been a consultant to the Carabinieri, than working with other conservators.

The difference will be that Vittorio's colleagues will take my opinions seriously."

Vittorio smiled wryly. "They'd better, if they know what's good for them. Flora is a force to be reckoned with."

Silvana sat down heavily at the table. "But what about getting married and having a family? Won't you two ever make time for that?"

Vittorio's smile lit his whole face. "Actually, we have news in that department."

Flora threw open her arms. "Mamma, Papa, we want to get married next Christmas. Here in Chicago. And we want Vittorio's parents to come too, of course."

Flora's mother transformed. "A wedding! To think I should see the day. Oh, that's wonderful!" She rose to stir her sauce, already talking about finding a venue for the reception and how many bridesmaids Flora would have. "Thank goodness you are staying all week, Flora! We can make a start." She turned on Flora. "And you, missy, are a sly one to pretend you weren't already planning a marriage!"

Flora laughed.

Ian shook Vittorio's hand and hugged his daughter. "Flora and Vittorio, you could not have told us anything that would please us more."

Flora beamed at Vittorio over her father's shoulder.

"Mission accomplished," she said.

Afterword

Today, the Uffizi Gallery of Florence is one of the best-protected museums in the world, with state-of-the-art alarm systems and restricted access. It is true, however, that the renovations that made it that way took place in multiple phases over many years. As you will see when you consult the New Uffizi website: http://www.uffizi.com/galleria-degli-uffizi/i-nuovi-uffizi.asp states, the object of the planning team was to keep the museum open to the public during as much of the work as possible. Renovations began immediately after World War II, experienced a major setback after the great flood of 1966, and proceeded up until June 2013 and later with the opening of two new staircase and elevator blocks, new offices, expanded restrooms and bookstore/gift shop, and better laboratory spaces.

This story takes place sometime before the opening of the Western (also called the Copper) Staircase, designed by Natalini and opened in December 2011.

In 2015-2016, the works of Botticelli were temporarily moved to Room 41 while lighting and air-conditioning systems were updated. By the time I visited the Uffizi for the third time in November 2016, those paintings were back in their preferred location of rooms 10-14. The new conservation laboratory is now in separate building in the

Boboli Gardens near the Pitti Palace, not on the first floor of the Uffizi as I describe in my novel.

I have taken artistic license with the floor plan (the real Uffizi has several more staircases and odd sections that jut out from the L-shaped footprint), timetable, and order of renovations, and deliberately set the story when the most extensive renovations were still in progress. Having worked myself in buildings under construction at the University of Illinois, I know just how confusing and distracting the noise and dust and continuous comings and goings can be to employees. For Flora and Vittorio and the Carabinieri, I wanted to maximize the atmosphere of chaos and the enormous difficulties of tracking all those employees, contractors, workmen, and potential art thieves.

My research was conducted in Italy, physical libraries, and online. For anyone interested in the subjects of art theft, antiquities smuggling, and art forgery, here are some of my favorite sources:

Eric Hebborn, The *Art Forger's Handbook*, 1997.

Noah Charney, *The Art of Forgery*, 2015 (his chapter headings are wonderful: "Genius," "Pride," "Revenge," "Fame," "Crime," "Opportunism," "Money," and "Power").

Roger Atwood, *Stealing History: Tomb Raiders, Smugglers, and the Looting of the Ancient World*, 2004.

Peter Watson and Cecilia Todeschini, *The Medici Conspiracy: The Illicit Journey of Looted Antiquities from Italy's Tomb Raiders to the World's Greatest Museums*, 2006.

Meet Sarah Wisseman

Sarah Wisseman is a retired archaeologist. Her experience working on excavations and in museums inspired two contemporary series, the Lisa Donahue Archaeological Mysteries and the Flora Garibaldi Art History Mysteries. Her settings are places where she has lived or traveled (Israel, Italy, Egypt, Massachusetts, and Illinois) and her favorite museum used to be housed in a creepy old attic at the University of Illinois.

Other Works From The Pen Of

Sarah Wisseman

The Dead Sea Codex - Two archaeologists working in Israel race to find an ancient manuscript about the teaching of Jesus' female disciples before Christian fanatics destroy it.

The Fall of Augustus - When Victor Fitzgerald is killed by a falling statue, Lisa Donahue becomes Interim Director of her Boston University museum. Suddenly she's juggling murder, artifact theft, and a complicated move into a new building. Then the treacherous Dean announces her replacement: a vicious woman from Lisa's past.

Catacomb - An art conservator and her policeman boyfriend search for a lost trove of Nazi-looted art under Rome.

Visit Our Website

For The Full Inventory

Of Quality Books:

Wings ePress, Inc
https://wingsepress.com/

Quality trade paperbacks and downloads

in multiple formats, in genres

ranging from light romantic comedy

to general fiction and horror.

Wings has something for every reader's taste.

Visit the website, then bookmark it.

We add new titles each month!

Wings ePress Inc.
3000 N. Rock Road
Newton, KS 67114

CPSIA information can be obtained
at www.ICGtesting.com
Printed in the USA
LVHW082039191119
637872LV00013B/1465/P

9 781613 096086